Robert Mu

OHIO SHORT HISTORIES OF AFRICA

This series of Ohio Short Histories of Africa is meant for those who are looking for a brief but lively introduction to a wide range of topics in African history, politics, and biography, written by some of the leading experts in their fields.

Steve Biko
by Lindy Wilson

Spear of the Nation (Umkhonto weSizwe): South Africa's Liberation Army, 1960s–1990s
by Janet Cherry

Epidemics: The Story of South Africa's Five Most Lethal Human Diseases
by Howard Phillips

South Africa's Struggle for Human Rights
by Saul Dubow

San Rock Art
by J.D. Lewis-Williams

Ingrid Jonker: Poet under Apartheid
by Louise Viljoen

The ANC Youth League
by Clive Glaser

Govan Mbeki
by Colin Bundy

The Idea of the ANC
by Anthony Butler

Emperor Haile Selassie
by Bereket Habte Selassie

Thomas Sankara: An African Revolutionary
by Ernest Harsch

Patrice Lumumba
by Georges Nzongola-Ntalaja

Short-changed? South Africa since Apartheid
by Colin Bundy

The ANC Women's League: Sex, Gender and Politics
by Shireen Hassim

The Soweto Uprising
by Noor Nieftagodien

Frantz Fanon: Toward a Revolutionary Humanism
by Christopher J. Lee

Ellen Johnson Sirleaf
by Pamela Scully

Ken Saro-Wiwa
by Roy Doron and Toyin Falola

South Sudan: A New History for a New Nation
by Douglas H. Johnson

Julius Nyerere
by Paul Bjerk

Thabo Mbeki
by Adekeye Adebajo

Robert Mugabe
by Sue Onslow and Martin Plaut

Robert Mugabe

Sue Onslow and Martin Plaut

OHIO UNIVERSITY PRESS

ATHENS

Ohio University Press, Athens, Ohio 45701
ohioswallow.com
© 2018 by Ohio University Press
All rights reserved

Printed in the United States of America
Ohio University Press books are printed on acid-free paper ⊗ ™

Cover illustration and design by Joey Hi-Fi

28 27 26 25 24 23 22 21 20 19 18   5 4 3 2 1

Library of Congress Cataloging-in-Publication Data
Names: Onslow, Sue, 1958- author. | Plaut, Martin, author.
Title: Robert Mugabe / Sue Onslow and Martin Plaut.
Other titles: Ohio short histories of Africa.
Description: Athens, Ohio : Ohio University Press, 2018. | Series:
Ohio short
   histories of Africa | Includes bibliographical references and index.
Identifiers: LCCN 2018000073| ISBN 9780821423240 (pb : alk.
paper) | ISBN
 9780821446386 (pdf)
Subjects: LCSH: Mugabe, Robert Gabriel, 1924- |
 Presidents--Zimbabwe--Biography. | Zimbabwe--Politics and
government--1980-
Classification: LCC DT3000 .O57 2018 | DDC 968.91051092--dc23
LC record available at https://lccn.loc.gov/2018000073

Contents

Illustrations

Maps

Plates

Following page 172

Tables

Abbreviations

Abbreviation	Full Name	Significance
ANC	African National Congress	South African liberation movement
AU	African Union	Successor of OAU since 2001 as the continental body uniting African states
CAF	Central African Federation	A short-lived British creation, uniting Northern and Southern Rhodesia [today Zambia and Zimbabwe] with Nyasaland [present day Malawi], 1953–63
CIO	Central Intelligence Organisation	Security Service founded by whites in 1964, but retained by Mugabe
FRELIMO	Frente de Libertação de Moçambique	Mozambican liberation movement
GPA	Global Political Agreement	Agreement to establish a coalition government of ZANU-PF and MDC, 2008
MDC	Movement for Democratic Change	Opposition party born out of trade unions and civil society organizations in 1999

OAU	Organisation of African Unity	Predecessor of the African Union as the continental body uniting African states in one organization, 1963–2002
SADC	Southern African Development Community	Founded April 1, 1980, the organization designed to unite independent African states in confronting the white government of South Africa; today mainly a regional developmental grouping
UDI	Unilateral Declaration of Independence	Independence from Britain by white Rhodesians, November 1965
ZANLA	Zimbabwe African National Liberation Army	ZANU's armed wing
ZANU	Zimbabwe African National Union	Mugabe's party, founded in 1963
ZANU-PF	Zimbabwe African National Union (Patriotic Front)	Mugabe's party after it united with Joshua Nkomo's ZAPU in 1987
ZAPU	Zimbabwe African People's Union	Led by Joshua Nkomo, founded in 1961
ZIPA	Zimbabwe People's Army	Short-lived attempt to unite the military wings of Zimbabwe's rival liberation movements, 1975
ZIPRA	Zimbabwe People's Revolutionary Army	ZAPU's armed wing

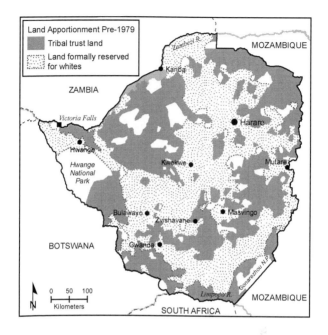

Map 1. Land apportionment pre-1979. Map by Brian Edward Balsley, GISP.

Map 2. June 2000 parliamentary elections. Map by Brian
Edward Balsley, GISP.

Introduction

On November 21, 2017, the Zimbabwean military forced President Robert Gabriel Mugabe to resign from office. At the age of ninety-three, he had been in power for thirty-seven years. He was worn down by the decades in office, falling asleep during official functions, and surrounded by sycophants. By the time he was overthrown, Mugabe appeared to be little more than an African despot, ruling via his security services and dominated by a much younger, rapacious wife who dreamed of succeeding him.

Yet Mugabe was, in reality, more than this caricature. His tragedy was that he stayed in office as leader of the country and head of his party, ZANU-PF,[1] for far too long. His real achievements had long since faded from public consciousness. When he finally resigned, there was a dominant public narrative of Zimbabwe as a tyrannical "basket case." Responsibility for this tragedy was laid squarely at his door. The truth is more complicated. Certainly, leadership in young African democracies has been a key factor in determining their postindependence trajectories. However, Zimbabwe's fortunes since independence cannot be distilled down to the attitude and actions of just one man. Mugabe, both as a dedicated leader within a liberation movement and as a political personality, was intricately linked to the outcome of the original struggle for independence and the end of white domination in 1980. He shaped the course of his country since independence, but Western misunderstanding of the importance of political cultures and structures of power in Zimbabwe has oversimplified the picture.

Robert Mugabe emerged as head of the political wing of one of the two main liberation movements—the Zimbabwe African National Union (ZANU)—through a combination of luck, guile, ideological focus, and persuasion. As prime minister, and later as president of Zimbabwe, Mugabe proved to be a master of "divide and rule." He had perfected these political skills while maneuvering between rival factions within his own movement then operating from external bases in neighboring Mozambique in the mid-1970s. Mugabe won the initially reluctant endorsement of the guerrilla fighters as they took on the army of the white regime. In 1979 Britain finally persuaded all the factions involved in the conflict to come to London for talks at Lancaster House. Mugabe still believed he could win the guerrilla war, and was reluctantly persuaded by African heads of state to accept British-supervised multiparty elections. The war-weary population, influenced by the infiltration of ZANU guerrillas, was persuaded of the attractions—as well as the necessity—of a victory for Mugabe's party in the 1980 independence elections. From then on, Mugabe worked to ensure the unquestioned dominance of his party and policies. In the mid-1980s he unleashed a violent campaign against the rival liberation movement, Zimbabwe African People's Union (ZAPU), and its leader, Joshua Nkomo. Thousands died in southwestern Zimbabwe, and Mugabe progressively arrogated more and more power to himself.

Mugabe's political and international reputation achieved its high point between 1987 and 1995. At the outset of Zimbabwe's independence, the country attracted remarkable international goodwill and a substantial injection of foreign funds, including British and Canadian financial support for a land reform program. There were dramatic improvements in education and primary health care. By the early 1990s, Mugabe had established an international political image and reputation as one of the senior successful national liberation leaders turned politicians, a pillar of the modern Commonwealth, and a key regional advocate for transition in neighboring South Africa. Mugabe's rhetoric of reconciliation and nation building, which was so striking to both the suspicious white population and the international community, faded as the years went on. He renewed calls for a continuation of the liberation struggle's goals. By the end of the 1990s, his star was in relative eclipse. His thwarted attempts to accelerate land reform and domestic austerity, along with mounting social and political challenges at home, caused Mugabe's popularity to decline, while his reputation was damaged on the international stage by the flawed decision to intervene in the war in the Democratic Republic of Congo.

As he had done before, and would do time and again in future under pressure from multiple quarters, Mugabe presented himself as the only solution to his movement, ZANU-PF's problems. At the same time, he buckled in the face of war veterans' demands for larger pensions—with disastrous financial results for the Zimbabwean public purse. Then Mugabe decided to answer calls for land redistribution by encouraging the initially haphazard invasion of mainly white-owned farms. From 2000 the country experienced a progressive economic meltdown and the growing militarization of government administration. Long accustomed to using violence as a political language, his party's leadership and security chiefs unleashed a program of abduction, beatings, and intimidation against the opposition and civil society activists.

By this point, the country was effectively being run by the security apparatus's Joint Operations Command. At the apex of these structures of state security sat Robert Mugabe with key elites who had a direct interest in sustaining his rule. These members of the military and security services refused to let Mugabe stand down following the 2008 election. Mugabe proved to be the ultimate political survivor, repeatedly outsmarting political rivals. When participating in a Government of National Unity from 2009 to 2013, Morgan Tsvangirai, the most serious political opponent to emerge since independence, found himself outmaneuvered by the veteran leader. Mugabe served the interests of the military, political, and business elites who kept him in power for nearly four decades, until they finally turned on him, fearful that he would install his wife, Grace, in the presidency.

As a man and a leader, Mugabe proved a deeply complex and contradictory individual. His character mixed qualities and vices in equal measure. Like Nelson Mandela, he was a "prison graduate," having spent ten years in a Rhodesian jail. The experience taught him remarkable self-possession. He could contain his anger at personal tragedy, but was deeply embittered by racial and social injustice in Rhodesia and its delayed transition to black majority rule. A highly intelligent and learned man—as Lord Carrington (the key British negotiator at the Lancaster House talks) once observed—he could be magnanimous when things were going his way, but vicious in adversity. His cabinet colleagues realized that resigning from office was not an option, as he could turn on them as potential political rivals. Instead, they should wait to be dismissed.

An intellectual shaped by his Jesuit education and his Marxist beliefs, there was a remarkable consistency to his thinking. Despite the fact that the rest of the world and the international political economy had moved on, he resolutely refused to do so. A bibliophile—even as Zimbabwe's leader—Mugabe would fly incognito to

London to browse the shelves of Dillon's bookshop. An eloquent and charismatic speaker, he tailored his message according to his audience, and ensured that his words resonated directly with the hopes and aspirations of his listeners. His particular outlook, his political skills, his dominance of his party, and his extraordinary longevity in office meant Robert Mugabe's personal history is woven through that of his country. The two cannot be separated.

Controversial and Divisive Leader

Robert Mugabe was head of the Zimbabwean liberation movement, the Zimbabwean African National Union (ZANU), then his country's first prime minister in April 1980. Zimbabwe had experienced a particularly tumultuous path to internationally recognized independence from formal British rule: from quasi-autonomous colonial status in 1923 as Southern Rhodesia; then as part of the decade-long experiment of the Central African Federation; and subsequently as Southern Rhodesia and the defiant attempt at white settler independence from London between 1965 and 1979. From the outset in 1980, his role as head of government, then executive head of state was an especially important variable in Zimbabwe's postindependence history. Addressing the challenges of colonial legacies and meeting expectations for development and progress placed particular demands on his vision, personal qualities, intellectual attributes, and ability to sustain necessary political alliances. None of this could be separated from the wider international environment. Western governments hoped Zimbabwe under Mugabe's leadership would represent a successful transition to multiracial, modified capitalism which could be held up as a model for neighboring apartheid South Africa. The Zimbabwean economy was the second-most-diversified economy in sub-Saharan Africa. At the independence celebrations, President Julius Nyerere of Tanzania advised Mugabe, "You have inherited a jewel. Keep it that way."[1] However, under Mugabe's leadership, the country advanced in some areas, only to lurch into cycles of crisis and decline, disappointing these early hopes.

Mugabe embodied the complexity and contradictions of Zimbabwe's history and political culture. At independence, his emphasis on racial and political reconciliation antedated President Nelson Mandela's call for national solidarity in South Africa in the 1990s. To the puzzlement of Western observers, Mugabe remained respected and revered by admirers across the African continent as a symbol of African liberation. "To many he is the embodiment of black pride, of achieving true psychological independence, of sticking two fingers up to the arrogant West."[2] This heroic status contrasted sharply—in the eyes of his many detractors—with repeated cycles of social and economic disruption, capital flight, mass unemployment, and emigration, precipitated by the policies of his government.

Since 2000, Zimbabwe's political economy has endured a roller-coaster ride, directly associated with the Fast Track Land Reform Programme (FTLRP). Following the short-lived stabilization of the economy between 2009 and 2014, there have been renewed socioeconomic problems, an acceleration of political protest via social media, and bitter factional infighting within the ruling party, ZANU-PF, over the presidential succession. Furthermore, Mugabe's leadership is rightly associated with the brutal repression of political opposition in the early years of independence. There have been repeated patterns of state-engineered violence and intimidation around election campaigns, and against individual political opponents, together with massive corruption and theft of Zimbabwean state assets. There is bitter historical irony in the fact that, just as in the period of Rhodesia's unilateral declaration of independence, Zimbabwe's fractured political and social landscapes since the 1990s have contributed to regional instability. For many, it is now difficult to remember Mugabe was once widely admired as a progressive leader, a respected chairman of the Non-Aligned Movement (1986–89), a leading Front Line States[3] president in the international struggle against apartheid, and a pillar of the Commonwealth in the 1980s and 1990s. There is also the bitter irony that Mugabe hosted the Commonwealth summit in 1991 which produced one of the key declarations of this international association, supporting democracy, good governance, human rights, and the rule of law.[4]

Although journalists and commentators remarked over the years that Mugabe "changed," the highly respected analyst Stephen Chan has pointed out that he was remarkably consistent in his outlook and ideological beliefs. Instead, it is the rest of the world which has moved on.

What of Mugabe's own ideological thinking and thought processes? Political commentators have debated whether Mugabe was an African nationalist, a determined socialist, a Marxist, or a Maoist in his ideological thinking.[5] "'Marxist'—The term is relative. . . . Mugabe made it clear in our discussions that his greatest mentor was Marshal Tito of Yugoslavia, the founder of the Non-Aligned Movement, from whom he had learned that adherence to communism does not necessarily mean subservience to Russia."[6] Mugabe was brought up in the Roman Catholic faith, but British intelligence realized he was not a practicing Catholic by the late 1970s, although his first wife, Sally Mugabe, herself a convert, regularly went to Mass. Arguably, there are elements of all these ideological and values-based influences in his outlook, which have endured to the present day. As leader of the revolutionary movement, the Zimbabwe African National Union (ZANU), he certainly impressed journalists that he was persuaded by the egalitarian and redistributive qualities of socialism. Mugabe found Marxism to be a useful theoretical critique of white settler capitalism, as well as offering appropriate structures of linkages between party organization and the wider population. However, despite acute international concern over what were deemed to be his extreme Marxist views, at independence he did not seem to have been as committed to

Marxism as the radical nationalist leadership in neighboring Mozambique or Angola.[7]

Mugabe's earlier ideas and advocacy of "developmental nationalism" hardened through the years of crisis and decline in the 1990s and 2000s into a narrower version of Afro-radicalism and nativism, with its reliance on cultural nationalism. This was not a rejection of his earlier ideological outlook, but rather a reinvigoration, which drew increasingly upon "an exclusionary and more adversarial imagery of the nation."[8] The Fast Track Land Reform Programme (see chapter 5) encapsulated his view of state prescriptions combining with popular mobilization to reinforce a particular version of Zimbabwean national identity. This then was a question of "changing deployment and articulation of nationalism."[9]

Mugabe's Afro-radicalism was purposive—as a state ideology, and also as a self-serving political imagination for a specific elite. This was not a fixed construct, but susceptible and available for manipulation and control. (It must be said Mugabe himself was remarkably consistent in his arguments.) In Mugabe's case, this articulation of Zimbabwean nationalism—referred to as "patriotic blackness" by some commentators[10]—enabled him to reenergize his links and support among the people (the *"povo"*). It also provided an alternative legitimacy and countermanding narrative to multiracial liberalism and cosmopolitanism, typified by the challenge of the Movement for Democratic Change (MDC) and its supporters. In this mind-set, the MDC represents a re-gressive, counterrevolutionary, "neocolonial" force, and one that must be resisted at all cost. This mirrors the paradox at the heart of other postcolonial transformations by national liberation movements elsewhere in Southern Africa. In Mugabe's case, his thinking typified a vision which combines radicalization and embourgeoisement, satisfying the Zimbabwean dispossessed and their demands for social justice, and the vested interests of ZANU-PF party elite and its allies in their search for resource accumulation. In this version of the African national project, Zimbabwe will achieve national unity and solidarity. It demands the merger of party and state to wield control of the economy according to a narrative which privileges indigenous advancement, expressly to resist rollback by external, malign, "neocolonial" forces.

Under Mugabe's leadership, therefore, ZANU-PF's decolonization project was not simply a need; it was an entitlement. Thus, those who point out Mugabe did not understand the influences and importance of the forces of globalization on Zimbabwe—only one of his many degrees is in economics—miss the point. Other critics of his ideological thinking focused on his great age and outdated ideas—that by the age of ninety-three, his ideas of monopoly capitalism (formed in the 1950s and 1960s) and conviction of the autonomy of the party-state as paramount socioeconomic actor and driver of development did not correspond to the current international political economy. This outlook was also fundamentally out of step with the predominant thinking of international financial institutions and international money markets.

Mugabe's Afro-radicalism remained undaunted and undimmed. He remained intent on socioeconomic transformation and its intimately associated racial dimensions through redistributive justice and indigenization of the economy, forging unity and solidarity before moving then to the (increasingly distant) phase of social equity. While to his critics this way of thinking proved to be the ultimate disruptive "denial politics," and hypocritical in the extreme, to Mugabe, these ideological practices and tenets were entirely rational. His criteria had long been national assertion and identity, agency and status, and a rejection of Western "imperialist" knowledge cultures and neoliberal prescriptions. Everything should be focused on expunging the "colonial personality" of Zimbabwean state and society. This also was bound up in Mugabe's view of what now defines the nation, who is a citizen—and correspondingly, who is not—and ultimately, what comprises a "good Zimbabwean." This definition was intimately connected to belonging to a particular political community, participating in and endorsing the ZANU-PF project, with Mugabe as its leader and keeper of the flame of patriotic memory.[11]

Mugabe's Afro-radicalism should also be seen in a broader context beyond the domestic sphere, as it had direct implications for Zimbabwe's foreign policy during his time in power. Responsibility for foreign policy was concentrated in his office, and in his position as first prime minister then president. Mugabe's advocacy and standing in the Non-Aligned Movement in the 1980s was a deliberate attempt to chart a more independent course in Southern Africa in the Cold War era—a "rough neighborhood," given apartheid South Africa's counter-insurgency activities—which was equidistant between the superpower blocs. This was a concerted effort to give Zimbabwe greater room for maneuver and more influence on the international stage. Until 2003, he also used the postcolonial modern Commonwealth as a platform to promote Zimbabwe's national interests, and to criticize both the United States and the United Kingdom (particularly over the crisis of the American invasion of Grenada in 1983.) His Afro-radicalism was also bound up with his view of revitalized Pan-Africanism, manifest through the Southern African Development Community and the Organisation of African Unity (OAU) and its successor organization since 2001, the African Union (AU). (This determined assertion of African identity and entitlement in opposition to what he deemed to be Western imperialism, and Zimbabwe's own progressive diplomatic isolation, led him to collaborate actively with the maverick Libyan leader, Muammar Qaddafi, in the late 1990s and 2000s, with sinister consequences.[12]) Mugabe long regarded the AU's economic agenda, and its evolving peace and security architecture, through the lens of African postcolonial autonomy in the international community. This was an extension of expunging the "colonial personality" of international interference, aid, and assistance to the continent, involving "weaning" the AU from foreign donor support. Despite being Africa's oldest head of state, Mugabe was appointed chairman of the AU in 2015. His acceptance speech encapsulated his determination to ensure African control over its natural resources and to reduce foreign exploitation of its mineral wealth: "African resources should belong to Africa and to no one else, except to those we invite as friends. Friends we shall have, yes, but imperialists and colonialists no more."[13] (To Mugabe's chagrin, 60 percent of the AU's funding has come from international donors such as the World Bank, the European Union, and other individual Western governments.[14]) Mugabe's one-year appointment exasperated his many critics at home and in Western capitals, who felt it reflected poorly on the AU's agenda of good governance and human rights. However, after 1980 Mugabe refused to be deflected from his version of good government and African states' rights. He was indeed remarkably consistent in his arguments and approach.

As for his personal characteristics, Mugabe was supremely disciplined, and well into late middle age, would wake early, around 4:30 a.m., exercise, meditate, and then return to his books. This was a regime he established in his thirties in Ghana and maintained throughout his incarceration by the Rhodesian government, exile in Mozambique, and even after his election as prime minister and then president of Zimbabwe. This denotes determined self-control—using routine to instil order at the core of his daily life, even when surrounded by political turmoil, violent disorder, and upheaval. Unlike Nelson Mandela, Mugabe emerged from prison in the mid-1970s into an extraordinary degree of factional infighting within his movement, tumultuous liberation politics, and regional criticism and dissent. He therefore faced intense challenges which required remarkable personal resilience, inner conviction, the ability to marshal a disciplined team, and a ruthless determination to exploit weakness and opportunity.

Over the years his political opponents repeatedly described Mugabe as intellectual but withdrawn, emotionally cold but with extraordinary personal energy. On first meeting him in Lusaka in December 1974, his domestic opponent Bishop Abel Muzorewa characterized him as slender and intense: "He was quite the opposite of the imagined big-shouldered militant."[15] British foreign secretary David Owen, his political antagonist in the 1970s, likened him to "a coiled spring, tense and very prickly and also somewhat withdrawn."[16] "Reserved, almost shy in manner, Mugabe at first impression seemed more cut out for the priesthood than for leadership of a political party. This was soon belied by his formidable intelligence and steely determination."[17] Another British foreign secretary, Lord Carrington, was struck by his poise and lack of bitterness at his long imprisonment. "I am not bitter against people personally. . . . But I am bitter against the system, the regime."[18] He impressed

Swedish officials in 1977 (whom he was approaching for substantial financial support) as a humble, soft-spoken, and intelligent man—the very opposite of the expected popular stereotype of a guerrilla leader as "fierce, rugged, pugnacious, bombastic and permeated through and through with megalomania."[19]

In contrast to this moderate picture, as a leader post-1980, he came across as "very opinionated." President Ronald Reagan found their encounter in 1983 rather trying: "He talked a monologue for 20 mins. Got round to our—as he put it—intervening in Angolan affairs because of our effort to get Cuba out of Angola. Then moved to El Salvador and Nicaragua. I caught him taking a breath and interrupted." Reagan noted tartly that Zimbabwe had by that point voted against the USA in the UN even more than the Soviets.[20]

However, great liberation fighters are not necessarily great nation builders,[21] and Mugabe was not even a proven combatant in the liberation war. This placed him at a disadvantage in the eyes of the proven guerrilla commanders, and those who were more radical in their outlook within the ZANU-PF Central Committee. Once in power, did Mugabe display "transformative leadership," showing courage, integrity, and intellectual honesty? The following chapters will argue that at times, the answer is "yes," although Mugabe lacked emotional intelligence and capacity for empathy. Over his long political career he demonstrated a remarkable ability to keep certain constituencies on side, to mobilize and inspire them. To his chagrin, he was regarded as a lesser leader than Nelson Mandela—he certainly did not provide responsible and enlightened leadership in the Western sense. It is fair to describe his as an amoral style of leadership, but also a curiously hybrid one, with its emphasis on anti-imperialism, constitutional forms, and electoral legitimacy. There is a long-lasting cult of respect for his leadership among some Zimbabweans, although he was ultimately responsible for unleashing periods of ruthless violence to solidify and perpetuate ZANU-PF's rule. His love of Savile Row suits, admiration for the British monarch,[22] and cultivated British accent when speaking English sat oddly with his vehement denunciation of British imperialism and interference in Zimbabwe's sovereign affairs.

Over the course of his long political career, Mugabe fell out with all of his former radical nationalist allies and colleagues. His relationship with his rival as a nationalist leader, Joshua Nkomo, was also fraught with difficulty throughout the liberation struggle period. Their mutual antagonism degenerated into bitter recrimination in the 1980s, before Nkomo's party ZAPU was subsumed into ZANU-PF in 1987. Unlike the less charismatic Mugabe, Nkomo had the "quality of the common touch" and approachability.[23] Within the ZANU-PF hierarchy, Mugabe progressively fought with his former comrades, who became his most vocal critics (see chapter 8). As his former ZANU colleague Ibbo Mandaza has pointed out, plotters within ZANU-PF tried to unseat their leader since at least the 1980s,[24] yet his version of electoral autocracy continues to triumph. Contemporary observers felt the death of his first wife, Sally, in early 1992, removed a crucial restraining influence on his political outlook.[25] In recent years Mugabe's relationship with a core coterie within the ZANU-PF Politburo was underpinned by his connections with his own ethnic subgroup, the Zezuru. This "trust" network became increasingly important with the passage of time and his advancing age. His grip on power went beyond personalized control, as these connections provided mutually reinforcing patrimonial networks. These informal networks also fed into the formal institutions of the state, as the judiciary, the executive, the administration, and business have been progressively co-opted by party control and patronage. This matrix of relationships is compounded by the militarization of state administration since 2000.[26] Mugabe sat at the apex of this pattern of power and privilege, which represents the "ZANU-fication" of the Zimbabwean state.

To his neoliberal detractors, then, Mugabe poses an object lesson in the dangers of political elites trying to pursue economic policies or developmental models in isolation from the international political economy. At home, Mugabe's attachment to election processes to legitimate his party's continued political preeminence was paralleled by his willingness to license violence to achieve political goals. A conviction politician dedicated to the decolonization of Zimbabwean society, he remained constant to his belief in redistribution in the name of the *povo* and in the likelihood of malign agency of hostile Western imperialist and neocolonial forces. His example and message still have considerable contemporary resonance in South Africa, while even his African critics privately admire his successful defiance of Western lecturing. As a political persona, he represented a complex amalgam of European ideological thinking of revolutionary transformation and Zimbabwean ethnic and cultural particularism. His stress on nationalist ideology and its particular version of Zimbabwean black nationalism combined with a vast network of corruption and patronage. This represents a fusion of a nationalist transformation agenda, an enduring authoritarian political culture inherited from the "white settler" colonial period, "spoils politics" of greed and corruption, and the expedient use of the security apparatus. Mugabe was part of the "complex picture of how individuals and groups became bound up in the project of state- and nation-building, despite contesting or even rejecting aspects of it."[27] In sum, he embodied the dictum: l'Etat, c'est moi.

2

Birth of the Revolutionary

Mugabe's formative years in colonial Southern Rhodesia had a lasting influence on his political beliefs. He was born on February 21, 1924, at the small Roman Catholic Kutama Mission in the impoverished Zvimba Communal area, about fifty miles outside the colonial capital, Salisbury. He was the third surviving child of Bona and Gabriel Mugabe. His maternal grandparents were farmers from the Zezuru community, which forms part of the wider Shona people.[1] Biographers have emphasized the modest circumstances of his childhood and his father's abandonment of the family in search of work in Bulawayo following the death of his older brother in 1934. At the age of nine, Robert Mugabe became the nominal man of the household. The departure of his father cemented his devotion to his mother. Bona Mugabe imbued her son with the sense that he was destined for great things, and consistently stressed the importance of education and learning—much respected in Zimbabwean culture as the means of personal and familial advancement. The importance of learning was matched by her emphasis on the importance of faith.

The Catholic fathers, too, exerted a particular influence on the young Mugabe, not least according to the tenets of a Jesuit education: "Give me the boy and I will show you the man." His education instilled in Mugabe a strong sense of personal discipline, an extraordinary fluency and ability to articulate his ideas in English, a remarkable cultivated British accent, and a forensic ability to deconstruct arguments, find flaws, and pose counterarguments. As a child, Mugabe was bookish and a "loner." Commentators stress his lifelong love of study, the importance he always attached to education and learning. Indeed, Mugabe is still described by his ZANU-PF colleagues as "the headmaster"—which suggests a stern disciplinarian and austere authority figure. The habits of instruction, together with a conviction that ultimately he has all the right answers, clearly never left him. Others have emphasized his remarkably trained mind, harnessed to his ability to listen.[2] While he might not be intellectually brilliant,[3] he was certainly clever, with a Jesuitical feel for politics and maneuver.

As a young man, Mugabe was also shaped by the environment of racial discrimination in Southern Rhodesia, with its evident white minority privilege. The Southern Rhodesian state's particular brand of white settler capitalism and extensive white land ownership contrasted with the Cartesian logic of his Catholic education. (The Catholic fathers in Southern Rhodesia later became widely known for their criticism of white minority rule and the violence associated with the state's counterinsurgency campaign in the Rhodesia UDI period. This led the Catholic fathers toward active support for Zimbabwean nationalism.) Therefore Mugabe was educated within an inspirational, rather than an institutional, church.[4] His mentor, Father Jerome O'Hea, also imbued him with a particular historical perspective of Irish nationalism and its long and ultimately victorious struggle against British imperial rule, partially achieved with the creation of the Irish state in 1922. During the Lancaster House conference in the autumn of 1979, Mugabe told a British delegate that he would like to pay his respects at Father O'Hea's grave.[5]

Mugabe's formative political experiences were also infused with the diverse political traditions of Zimbabwe's contested history and the development of the nationalist movement. Violence has long been embedded in the political landscape of the country. The Ndebele migration from South Africa led to the establishment of their hegemony over the existing peoples in the 1840s, continuing a pattern of "raiding, conquest, incorporation and assimilation of other communities, groups, and individuals as they migrated to the north."[6] Another surge of violence accompanied the arrival of the Pioneer Column, funded by the South African–based mining magnate, Cecil Rhodes. This led to the crushing of the Ndebele state. The subsequent Chimurenga wars of the 1890s, which united large sections of the Shona and Ndebele in revolt against white seizure of their land, were similarly victories for white colonial violence. In

1900, the defeat of the revolt by the Shona chief, Mapondera, meant that African resentment and attempts to dislodge colonial rule thereafter adopted a less confrontational approach.

A period of attempted accommodation followed, through "a proto-nationalist" period between the two world wars. During Mugabe's childhood and adolescence in the 1920s and 1930s, African political mobilization built upon self-help structures and activities of church groups and solidarity organizations. This political mobilization then moved into more formal structures of trade union organization (particularly within the Rhodesian railways and other state-run bodies) and voters' associations. These African organizations were relatively small-scale and focused on their own group interests, aiming their activities at securing concessions from the colonial administration rather than acting as a political voice for the black Zimbabwean masses. As protest organizations, they sought better government and the inclusion of their members in the colonial elite project. The most effective association in mobilizing mass support was the Rhodesian Industrial Commercial Workers Union, which agitated for better pay and conditions as well as against police harassment and the restrictive pass laws. However, in the 1930s "majority rule was a concept that neither the Africans nor the settlers entertained as a remote possibility. [White rule] seemed so entrenched at that point that few could doubt it as a fixed element of the natural order of creation."[7]

The failure of the Rhodesian colonial government to respond to emerging African political mobilization and these demands for accommodation radicalized African political consciousness. Change came in the post-1945 period. The Second World War acted as a catalyst, transforming the milder form of prewar "petition politics" for reform into more militant nationalism and mass mobilization. The 1950s saw demands for greater political representation and the removal of economic and residential discrimination. Politicized African soldiers in Southern Rhodesia were incensed that white soldiers were rewarded with land grants and generous financial support, whereas they had to return to the increasingly crowded African reserves and continued marginalization. African grievances were further aggravated by government displacement of rural communities to more arid and malarial areas to make way for white immigrants under the government-sponsored resettlement campaign.

This was also an era in which Southern Rhodesian society experienced dramatic change, with a rapidly expanding white population (from 30,000 in 1945 to 255,000 by 1965).[8] Class identity also played into the Southern Rhodesian social picture: the overwhelming majority of British migrants to Southern Rhodesia were ex-servicemen or economic migrants seeking an improved standard of living away from the grim austerity of postwar Britain. The country legalized job discrimination on the basis of color and limited African access to education. Furthermore, accelerated land alienation saw the additional eviction of over 100,000 Africans from their land. African grievances around land alienation were exacerbated by the appalling long-term conditions of African farmworkers on white-owned land. In addition, the expansion of the African urban workforce, a direct product of the country's industrialization and economic diversification, compounded problems of poor housing in the African urban settlement areas. These pressures were matched by rising demands for official recognition of workers' rights and trade union organization. There were also the daily humiliations of a racially divided and segregated society: separate queues in the post office, on buses and park benches, and at public amenities; and instances of racially motivated street harassment by white youth. As a youth, Mugabe had to endure the racial slurs and humiliations of colonial Rhodesia. Eddison Zvobgo, a childhood friend, described them both seeing the vicar's wife disinfecting the seat on which the young Mugabe and Zvobgo had been sitting, when invited to tea in form 4.[9]

Mugabe's world as a child and young man was therefore bound by racial and class hierarchies. His access to tertiary education and his employment prospects were consequently limited. He qualified as an elementary school teacher in 1941 and began teaching at Kutama in 1942, when he was eighteen. Coming from a relatively impoverished family, Mugabe did not have the means to apply to the University of Rhodesia. He worked briefly as a teacher at Garfield Todd's Dadaya New Zealand Churches of Christ Mission School in Midlands (where Ndabaningi Sithole was a fellow young teacher), earning the princely sum of £3.00 a month. Sponsored by his grandfather and Father O'Hea, Mugabe then spent two years at Fort Hare, the only black South African university, where he completed his teacher training education. There he met a number of South African black activists and was exposed to an extraordinary range of ideas of nationalist transformation and socialist modernity. These ideas emphasized black majority rule and the importance of state-directed development and centralized control of the economy. He was greatly influenced by ANC Youth Leaguers and the Africanist ideology of Anton Lembede. This was also his first encounter with Marxism, via contacts with the Communist Party of South Africa.

This was the era of the Central African Federation (CAF)—a decade-long British creation which fused the quasi-autonomous colony of Southern Rhodesia with the colonies of Northern Rhodesia and Nyasaland in 1953. This postcolonial federal experiment was short lived. As the 1950s progressed, the Conservative government in London was confronted by growing nationalist resentment within the CAF's composite parts. However, the CAF as an expanded economic area meant wider job opportunities for its inhabitants. Mugabe went to work in Northern Rhodesia, at a time of increasingly militant nationalism in Nyasaland and Northern Rhodesia against British colonial rule.

The catalyst of Mugabe's growing militancy was his move in 1958 to Ghana, where he worked at a teacher training college. As Mugabe later explained, "I went as an adventure. I wanted to see what it would be like in an independent African state."[10] He remained there for nearly three years, moving into the heady political climate of newly independent Ghanaian nationalism and of its charismatic leader, Kwame Nkrumah. It was also an era of considerable hope for African rapid "take-off" postindependence. In 1958, Mugabe attended the All African People's Conference in Accra, hosted by Nkrumah. The conference "openly declared independent Africa's support for the liberation struggles of colonised peoples of Africa."[11] Mugabe listened to Nkrumah speak in person on many occasions, and was inspired by his eloquent emphasis on "Pan-Africanism" as the means to "decolonise the African mind." Sally Hayfron, his colleague at Takoradi Teacher Training college and later his wife, remarked that their personal bond was grounded in their lengthy animated political discussions, shared outlook, and activism.

Mugabe's decision to return to Southern Rhodesia from Ghana in 1960 coincided with growing African nationalist dissent across the CAF, which heralded its dissolution in 1963. Spurred on by the success of African nationalist movements across the continent, Zimbabwean urban youth organization and trade union militancy, based in Bulawayo, fused to form the Southern Rhodesian African National Congress (SRANC) in

1958—soon known simply as the ANC. It was the first African/Zimbabwean political mass organization to demand black majority rule. Parallel attempts at accommodation by the African educated elite with the claimed "multiracial partnership" project and collaboration with white liberals, such as in the Inter-Racial Association and Capricorn Africa Society, were increasingly sidelined by this growing confrontational politics which fused urban youth resentment and trade union militancy with rural discontent.

Politics in Southern Rhodesia was becoming increasingly polarized. White resistance to accelerated black political and economic rights had already emerged in the late 1950s, in opposition to Prime Minister Garfield Todd, who was thought to be excessively sympathetic to African advancement. This white opposition was fueled by British prime minister Harold Macmillan's "wind of change" speech in Cape Town in February 1960 and its call for decolonization across sub-Saharan Africa. There was also the eruption of violence and descent into civil war in the Congo following Belgium's abrupt departure. The spectacle of lawlessness, attacks on remaining colonists, and white Congolese refugees camped on Salisbury showground entrenched white Rhodesian determination to ensure "responsible government" under white minority direction. Meanwhile, rising African nationalism combined with violent street demonstrations in Salisbury and Bulawayo resulted in a government crackdown, with the introduction of the Law and Order (Maintenance) Act which gave the Rhodesian authorities far-reaching powers of arrest and detention. Prime Minister Edgar Whitehead sought to bridge this divide with a drive for African advancement through a limited expansion of the franchise. The 1961 Constitution allowed for a modest advance of African voting rights through the creation of a complicated two-tier electoral roll. This constitution also proposed the election of fifteen African MPs to Parliament, but this was rejected by African nationalists. Whitehead also introduced a concerted drive to desegregate Rhodesian daily life, which proved deeply unpopular with the white electorate. A strong white backlash led to the victory of the reactionary Rhodesian Front in the December 1962 election. Ian Smith, a former fighter pilot with the Royal Air Force, emerged as a leading proponent of these right-wing policies.

This then was the febrile world of nationalist politics to which Mugabe returned from Ghana, on what was originally intended to be a short visit to his family. He was rapidly drawn into urban political activism. By now most members of the Zimbabwean nationalist elite rejected multiculturalism.[12] At this point Mugabe was very much in the mainstream of African nationalism, and was increasingly attracted to Marxist rhetoric of class antagonism. He was committed to the achievement of full black political rights, far-reaching economic redistribution, and Pan-Africanism. He threw himself into the Zimbabwean nationalist cause with the same single-minded fervor he had devoted to teaching. He was one of the first nationalists to advocate the shift to armed struggle, convinced that only this would overcome white resistance to the accelerated transfer of black political and economic rights. In 1961 he married Sally Hayfron, who matched her husband in her passion for politics and African advancement; she also shared his sense of injustice at colonial oppression and imperialist interference and control. By all accounts, theirs was a remarkable political marriage and a deeply affectionate personal relationship. Sally herself was intelligent, highly articulate, politically combative, and committed to the nationalist struggle. She also combined astute and instinctive judgment of character with shrewd political judgment and pragmatism, and was one of the very few people who could make Mugabe pause and reflect.

These were turbulent and fractious times in Zimbabwean urban politics. Within the next two years Zimbabwean nationalism went through three organizational name changes, culminating in the banning of the Zimbabwe African People's Union (ZAPU), then headed by trade union leader Joshua Nkomo. By this point the nationalist movement had made two important decisions: the shift to the acquisition of arms, sabotage, and ultimate armed confrontation to colonial rule; and the recruitment and military training of cadres overseas in Algeria, China, Czechoslovakia, Egypt, and Ghana. However, Zimbabwean nationalism was now also fatally fractured by personal rivalries and political difficulties, and the realities of an oppressive colonial state with greater force at its disposal. Mugabe had been one of those who criticized Nkomo's initial acceptance of the 1961 constitutional proposals in London as unlikely to accelerate African political rights. In 1963 ZAPU split into two parties with the creation of a new nationalist party, the Zimbabwe African National Union (ZANU). Unhappy with Joshua Nkomo's leadership, a group led by the Reverend Ndabaningi Sithole broke away and formed this rival political movement. Mugabe was appointed secretary general on the ZANU Central Committee.[13]

As the Central African Federation was breaking into its constituent parts and moving to independence as Zambia and Malawi, Zimbabwean nationalism's drive for black majority rule fractured into two deeply hostile and embittered political movements with limited appeal beyond the urban environment. The rival movements confronted each other on the streets. They also faced a repressive colonial state and its powerful security apparatus (the majority of whom were black). The white minority government in Salisbury collaborated with tribal chiefs in the rural areas who were determined not to see any erosion of their authority and control by their wayward "children." The political imagination of Rhodesia/Zimbabwe was thus a fractured and conflicted map of class, ethnic, linguistic, and racial divides. However, each African nationalist movement was focused on "a cult of unity"—"the obsession of African

44

nationalist politicians with what they see as the vital need to present a united front," which led directly to hostility to opposition.[14] At this stage ZAPU remained the larger nationalist force, and Joshua Nkomo was by now well known internationally. Small groups of ZANU fighters were sent abroad for training (to Egypt, Ghana, the People's Republic of China, and Tanzania), but their political campaign had little actual impact inside Zimbabwe, as there was no base from which they could operate inside the country.

The political tide was moving against Mugabe and his fellow nationalists. The election of the Rhodesian Front, followed by Ian Smith's appointment as Rhodesian prime minister in April 1964, and then the advent of the Labour government in the United Kingdom in October 1964, set London and Salisbury on a collision course. This led directly to Rhodesia's unilateral declaration of independence (UDI) in November 1965. Smith and his Rhodesian Front colleagues were "white ostriches" who infuriated Prime Minister Harold Wilson and his civil servants. In the meantime, Mugabe and his colleagues in ZANU looked to London to stop Smith, if necessary by force. Ironically, at this point the UK high commissioner identified ZANU as the party more likely to reach some sort of negotiated settlement with the Rhodesian government, and even contemplated sending covert British funds to support the organization.[15] Nothing came of this idea, as London concluded African nationalism inside Rhodesia "remains divided, frustrated, proscribed and without a single national leader of real stature."[16]

International African solidarity was to be an important component in Zimbabwean radical nationalism's eventual victory in 1980. In 1963, the Organisation of African Unity set up the Liberation Committee, based in Dar-es-Salaam, to provide diplomatic and logistical support, as well as funding and publicity for all the liberation movements recognized by the OAU. However, the African heads were bitterly divided on the best method and strategy. Crucially, it was ZAPU which was recognized as one of the "Authentic Ones." In the run-up to UDI, the OAU offered diplomatic solidarity and support: the first OAU meeting of African heads of state denounced an impending declaration of independence by the Southern Rhodesian government, and also called for the immediate release of African nationalist detainees. Africa's leaders looked to Britain to stop the slide toward UDI, and to use force if necessary, but were sorely disappointed.

In August 1964 both ZANU and ZAPU were banned, and along with other Zimbabwean radicals, Mugabe was arrested "for subversive speech" and imprisoned. (Sally Mugabe was briefly detained for political protest in 1964.) He remained in prison for the next decade. When Wilson visited Salisbury in October 1965, in a last throw of the dice to prevent a unilateral declaration of independence, he insisted on meeting the jailed African nationalist leaders. As the third-ranking ZANU member,

Mugabe was included in the ZANU group which met the British prime minister. Wilson argued that the threat of economic sanctions was an appropriate alternative political lever to prevent the Rhodesian government's defiance of London and the international community.[17] To the African nationalists, sanctions were a farce and would not succeed.[18] The director of the Rhodesian Central Intelligence Agency, Ken Flowers, later recalled that Wilson's statement gave the Rhodesian cabinet their opportunity; there was a meeting within hours of Wilson's press conference, on November 1, 1965, which confirmed the decision to go for UDI.

The Labour government resolutely refused to launch a military strike against the white settler rebel government. London felt it was simply incapable of asserting its authority over the Smith government.[19] This was the product of a combination of geopolitical, military, and domestic factors: logistical difficulties; the relative strength of the Rhodesian armed forces, which had inherited the CAF's modern air capability; profound concern over the reliability of British pilots and troops being asked to fight the white settler government, which had supported Britain in World War II and included many ex-service men; and concern over the possibility of wider racial war. Rhodesian UDI was also a fraught domestic political issue, and the Labour government only enjoyed a parliamentary majority of four. Furthermore, the Labour government had considerable doubts about the divided Zimbabwe nationalist movements.

In all, Wilson's government did not believe that it possessed the "dispassionate constitutional power to hold the ring ... to prevent the ambitions of the two communities reaching their present state of uncompromising mutual hostility."[20] Sanctions instead were regarded as the least bad option and—as Wilson argued—would bring the Rhodesian Front to heel "in a matter of weeks, if not months." This was a grave miscalculation. In 1966, with the backing of the UN Security Council, Britain did send ships of the Royal Navy to enforce a blockade off the Mozambican coast. The "Beira Patrol" (1966–75) had only a limited effect on Rhodesia, since oil and other key commodities continued to be imported via Lourenço Marques (Maputo) and South Africa.[21]

For the next decade Rhodesia seemed a defiant success story. Prior preparation by the Rhodesian government, South African financial and commercial collaboration and communications, and trading links through neighboring Portuguese-controlled Mozambique ensured that the rebel regime successfully defied international sanctions. Import substitution policies also boosted the Rhodesian economy, which enjoyed 7 percent growth until the mid-1970s. Sitting in Gonakudzingwa detention camp, close to the railway line to Portuguese Mozambique, detained nationalists could see sanctions-busting oil shipments from Lourenço Marques rolling toward Salisbury (now Harare). In 1966 and 1968 the small incursions of guerrillas from Zambia into the arid and sparsely populated Zambezi valley were rapidly crushed by the well-equipped and better-trained Rhodesian security forces. Following the failure of further negotiations with the British government on HMS *Tiger* and HMS *Fearless* in 1966–68, the Rhodesian Front government seemed to be riding high.

The years from 1964 to 1974 were therefore bleak ones for Mugabe and his fellow detainees. He had no hope of being released, but regarded his imprisonment as a necessary sacrifice for the liberation struggle and generations coming after him. For much of this time, he was held in prison in Salisbury with fellow ZANU dissidents Maurice Nyagumbo and Edgar Tekere; the three adjacent cells opened out onto a confined, covered concrete exercise area approximately 20ft x 40ft. The prisoners whiled away time by a rigorous routine of exercise, academic study, and impassioned discussions on politics. Mugabe completed two university degrees at the University of London (by correspondence course) while he was in jail. These were also years of personal tragedy. His young son died of cerebral malaria in Ghana in 1966, and he was refused permission to travel to the funeral. He was allowed personal letters, although these were always vetted by the prison authorities. Sometimes it proved possible to smuggle messages.

In the meantime, the liberation struggle was moving on without him. Under Herbert Chitepo, a military alliance was gradually established with FRELIMO from 1968, and in 1970 a front was opened in Tete Province, Mozambique. The ZANU leadership in exile undertook a detailed review of the movement's political and military activities, in conjunction with Chinese military instructors. This emphasized the importance of political preparation of guerrillas and the rural population in target areas before launching a guerrilla campaign, as the keys to success. Consequently, conventional incursions were rejected in favor of a phased and gradual build-up of revolutionary activity, using the countryside to encircle the towns. The attack on Altena Farm in December 1972 marked a new phase in ZANU's armed struggle as its guerrillas began infiltrating northeastern Rhodesia. Sixteen months later, the Portuguese "Carnation Revolution" in Lisbon in April 1974, the associated collapse of Portuguese colonial rule in southern Africa and acceleration of Mozambique's independence under the FRELIMO liberation movement was to prove a regional geopolitical earthquake. Now the Salisbury government was confronted by a porous border 1,500 kilometers long and by growing guerrilla attacks and infiltration into tribal trust lands and rural areas. Prodded by the South African government, the Rhodesian government embarked on talks with African nationalists.

Mugabe's contribution to the liberation struggle over the next five years (1974–79) should be seen as one particular piece of the jigsaw of radical Zimbabwean nationalism, rather than "the answer" to this complex picture. He emerged only gradually as the principal political spokesperson for ZANU, arguably more because of the flaws and failings of his rivals than for his own dynamic, charismatic leadership. Mugabe also won only reluctant endorsement from African presidents. His appointment as political leader of ZANU in August 1974 was the product of prison politics and profound disillusionment with the party leadership. The willingness of the Reverend Ndabaningi Sithole to enter into talks with the Smith government was greeted with disgust by the ZANU detainees and culminated in Mugabe's nomination as leader. But no one outside Que Que prison knew him.[22]

Ironically, Mugabe owed his "break" to Ian Smith. Mugabe was "temporarily" released from prison in late 1974 to attend the "unity" talks in Lusaka. This international summit between African nationalist leaders and Ian Smith was backed by the leaders of the Front Line States, with the involvement of the South African prime minister, B. J. Vorster, in the hope that an international settlement could accelerate the transfer to black majority rule. However, Mugabe was clearly determined not to compromise with the Rhodesian Front government, as his loathing of colonialism was undiminished. Talks were "too early," and he bitterly resented what he regarded as African heads of state "selling us out." He agreed only under duress to go to Zambia for a preliminary meeting.

The Lusaka summit in December 1974 was a heated and divisive affair. Mugabe was not a popular choice to lead his political movement. President Nyerere of Tanzania was particularly trenchant in his criticism of

Mugabe's unsuitability. Nyerere was furious at the idea of a ZANU leader sent to Lusaka with the Rhodesian government's connivance. He refused to talk to Mugabe, and demanded he return to Rhodesia and only come back with Sithole. Sithole himself rapidly agreed to a unity pact with ZAPU. Fractures continued within the party leadership: while appearing to yield to concerted Front Line States' pressure for a united front and to enter into negotiations with the Smith government, Mugabe and a narrow circle of trusted friends made clandestine plans for a recruitment drive for ZANU's military wing—ZANLA—now based inside Mozambique. These activities soon aroused the attention of the Rhodesian security forces, who had only reluctantly released Zimbabwean political prisoners as part of a South African–Zambian backed amnesty. In April 1975 Edgar Tekere and Mugabe used their sympathetic Catholic networks to make a hurried escape into Mozambique.[23]

Mugabe's ten-year incarceration had stiffened his determination to establish an egalitarian people's state. But the signs were far from auspicious. As a political liberation movement, ZANU had been experiencing profound internal conflicts, exacerbated by personality, ideology, and ethnicity. These culminated in the assassination of the ZANU national chairman and leader of ZANU's external supreme council, Herbert Chitepo in Lusaka in March 1975. Convinced that Chitepo had been the victim of internal party conflicts, the Zambian authorities rounded up leading ZANU figures they believed were implicated in his death. (In fact, the Rhodesian security forces were responsible.) This political crisis and Ndabaningi Sithole's "de facto non-leadership" of the ZANU rump in Zambia had repercussions for the movement's military wing, ZANLA, now based in Mozambique, where Mugabe was now trying to assert his political authority. There was a short-lived attempt to unite the military wings of the rival liberation movements (ZANU and ZAPU) into ZIPA (the Zimbabwe People's Army). African leaders hoped that under veteran military commander Rex Nhongo (the *nom de guerre* of Solomon Mujuru) ZIPA would gradually lead to the withering away of the competing factions led by Mugabe, Sithole, and Nkomo. However, within twelve months ZIPA had itself unraveled. The collapse of this joint military effort meant that for the rest of the liberation war, the two rival liberation movements fought parallel campaigns, ZANU based in Mozambique and ZAPU based in Zambia. Although nominally politically collaborating under a Patriotic Front umbrella, the movements were in reality bitter opponents. Mugabe was particularly critical of Nkomo's decision to keep most of his forces in Zambia, while ZANU fighters attacking from bases in Mozambique were dying in clashes with better-armed and better-trained white-led soldiers inside Rhodesia.

Mugabe was not responsible for the shift of the liberation struggle to guerrilla war based on rural mobilization. This had taken place under Chitepo's leadership, and as a tactic, it was to prove decisive in the outcome of the nationalists' conflict with the Rhodesian State.[24] Mugabe's initial plan upon arriving in Mozambique had been to build up a following for his position as leader of ZANU in the refugee camps. However, the Mozambique nationalist leader Samora Machel—who was initially very suspicious of Mugabe, whom he first regarded as a possible Smith agent—put him under house arrest in Quelimane (a port city over 1,500 kilometers north of the capital Maputo) "to keep him out of trouble."[25] In Machel's view, leaders of an armed struggle should emerge from the guerrilla ranks. Machel's distrust of Mugabe only dissipated slowly—the youthful ZIPA fighters named him as a possible alternative leader to Sithole, since they regarded Sithole as "completely hopeless and ineffectual"; but they didn't really know him.[26] Ironically, just as Machel was very reluctantly shifting to support Mugabe as the ZANU political representative, the youthful guerrilla fighters who had contributed to his rise were poised to reject him. Mugabe's leadership style and ideological orientation had profoundly alarmed the fighters. Their leader (himself the former leading ZANLA political commissar) Wilfred Mhanda later reflected, "It became obvious very quickly that we'd made a terrible mistake . . . that he was arrogant, paranoid, authoritarian and ruthless, a man believing only in power."[27] A group of several hundred party cadres— some of whom were in Tanzania—were detained and some were murdered. Outspoken criticism of Mugabe following the massive loss of life in the Rhodesian raid at Chimoio in November 1977 was ruthlessly suppressed by ZANLA military leaders Tongogara and Nhongo. In this way, Mugabe succeeded in incarcerating and containing his youthful critics.

Equally important to fighting this protracted and increasingly brutal liberation struggle was the responsibility for carrying the struggle to the outside world. It was a slow process. Having been in jail since 1964, Mugabe had little domestic or international visibility. In terms of reaching an audience inside Rhodesia, the *Voice of Zimbabwe* was broadcast over Radio Mozambique every evening. Together with guerrilla infiltration and indoctrination, this was a key means of rural mobilization and the Rhodesians regularly sought to jam these transmissions.[28] (The increasingly brutal behavior of the Rhodesian counterinsurgency forces, and forced displacements under the Protected Villages Scheme, also served to alienate many in the rural areas.) The *Zimbabwean News*—ZANU's official publication— had a regular, if small, circulation. Unlike his later fellow "jail graduate," Nelson Mandela, Mugabe did not benefit from a sustained campaign by the international Anti-Apartheid Movement identifying him as the iconic figure of Zimbabwean nationalism. He owed his rise in international awareness to information networks and personal sympathy for national liberation movements among radical Commonwealth leaders. Thanks to Jamaican prime minister Michael Manley's personal invitation, it was Nkomo who was able to speak to Commonwealth leaders in closed session at the Kingston Commonwealth Heads of Government meeting in Jamaica in April 1975. The creation of the Patriotic Front (a nominal political alliance of his movement with Joshua Nkomo's ZAPU) in October 1976 was only thanks to pressure from Tanzanian president Julius Nyerere, who was determined that Zimbabwean nationalism should present a united opposition during the constitutional talks in Geneva.

By the autumn of 1976 Mugabe was gradually gaining international recognition as the political leader of ZANU, even if he remained a relative unknown quantity. He was chosen to lead the ZANU delegation to the Geneva conference and insisted his colleagues be released from Zambian jails. As a liberation leader, Mugabe had no experience of diplomatic negotiations—skills which the Commonwealth secretary general, Shridath ("Sonny") Ramphal, realized were notably lacking. Consequently, the Commonwealth Secretariat provided constant administrative support for the Zimbabwe liberation delegations throughout the three-month-long fractious meeting in Geneva. Puzzled CIA and M16 surveillance reports compared notes on whether Mugabe was a Soviet "client" and concluded that the Soviet legation in Geneva was as much in the dark as diplomatic intelligence in London and Washington. His austere style and demeanor contrasted sharply with the established figure of Zimbabwean nationalism, *bon viveur*

Joshua Nkomo, who was known to rely on the financial largesse of the chairman of the Lonrho mining group, Tiny Rowland, and on his willingness to provide air transport. Gradually developing international contacts, Mugabe managed to persuade his international listeners that ZIPA was under ZANU's control—rather than the other way around.[29] However, the Geneva conference broke up in acrimony in late 1976, and Mugabe was obliged to return to exile in Mozambique.

From Freedom Fighter to President of a One-Party State

Mugabe spent the next three years based in Maputo. His wife, Sally, who had been in London from 1970, lobbying for the ZANU nationalist cause, had already joined him in Mozambique in 1975. An immensely loyal and practical person who understood the symbolism of politics, she threw herself into providing practical support for the liberation struggle—such as securing cloth and sewing machines from donors, and even making clothes herself for combatants and refugees. Gestures such as these ensured she was seen "as a caring and concerned person who was doing her best to alleviate the suffering of the freedom fighters and refugees."[1] This was an important boost to her husband's political popularity.

These were difficult times for ZANU. Gaining President Machel's support was only one of Mugabe's problems. ZANU's fighters remained short of funds for weaponry, food, and supplies in the field. The Chinese remained the main source of support for Mugabe's political and military movement throughout the liberation struggle.[2] Although Beijing did not supply vast quantities of sophisticated heavy weaponry, it did provide substantial shipments of small arms, mines, and explosives. However, these were inadequate, and by the late 1970s Mugabe was obliged to look for additional support from socialist countries. He was repeatedly rebuffed by the Soviet Union and the East Germans (the GDR), who regarded ZANU as a "splitist organization" unworthy of aid, but did get arms from North Korea, Romania, and Yugoslavia. Similarly, Mugabe bitterly resented continued Soviet pressure for a merger with ZAPU (led by his rival, Joshua Nkomo) after 1976, as well as Moscow's criticism for describing Mugabe as a "Marxist-Leninist of Maoist thought."[3] He developed an antagonism toward the Soviet Union for its insensitivity and insulting refusal to accord him recognition. While ZANU was doing most of the fighting, Moscow further alienated Mugabe by denying ZANU sophisticated weaponry, while channeling weapons to ZAPU forces (which were largely sitting idle in Zambia). Mugabe's ideological and military indebtedness to Beijing and his enduring suspicion of Moscow considerably influenced Zimbabwe's foreign relations postindependence.[4]

Meanwhile, ZANU's rival liberation movement, ZAPU, based in Zambia, received the lion's share of international support through the OAU, the Soviet bloc, and the Anti-Apartheid Movement's international network. Mugabe remained determined to ensure that ZANU was not absorbed into Nkomo's organization, while quashing all attempts to challenge his leadership.

Having gained international exposure at the abortive Geneva conference, Mugabe ordered the arrest of 600 fighters in ZANU's military wing, ZANLA, to prevent a possible military rebellion. The 64 top commanders were detained, in appalling conditions, until February 1980, when they were released on Lord Carrington's insistence under the Lancaster House settlement.

By March 1977, Mugabe was formally declared president of ZANU and leader of the guerrilla movement at a ZANU Central Committee meeting. This endorsement by his colleagues (and crucially the top military commanders) marked the beginning of the "Mugabe era," and the cult of the leader, "Comrade Robert Mugabe." It also saw his short-lived domination of the guerrilla war phase. Tekere later characterized Mugabe's behavior as "very insecure" and described his "need to be surrounded by admirers" because "this make him feel stronger and more assured"[5]—combined with aptitude for domination and control, using divide-and-rule tactics.[6] It was an environment in which Mugabe was surrounded by people vying for power and seeking favors. Tekere commented that Mugabe "didn't expect his word to be final at the beginning. But he began to like the idea." It was the start of the Mugabe personality cult.[7]

Under his leadership, ZANU was restructured and reorganized, with the establishment of a new Central Committee. Mugabe brought in a new cohort of university graduates from the Zimbabwean diaspora in Europe and proposed a two-phase revolutionary struggle: first, a nationalist revolution with the over-throw of the white state, then a socialist revolution.[8] Internal and external discipline was vital—and was seen as requiring unalloyed loyalty. Dissension was regarded as rebellion.[9] Using the Leninist concept of "democratic centralism," Mugabe insisted that power had to be focused and concentrated. In practice, this resulted in a narrow leadership group where the leader had the final say. He won FRELIMO's support, as Samora Machel was also preaching centralized control.[10]

Mugabe continued to face tensions with the ZANLA military leadership,[11] but he succeeded in winning the support of ZANLA "old guard" guerrilla commanders Nhongo and Josiah Tongogara, who shared his profound and enduring hostility toward ZAPU. ZANU made Mugabe commander in chief of the military wing, ZANLA.[12] The formal links between the two were through ZANU's "war council," itself dominated by civilians, not guerrilla fighters. The military wing's penetration of Rhodesia was organized by geographic sector and broken down into detachments and section commanders. This meant that ZANLA, despite the poor quality of its armaments and often lamentable training of its guerrillas, possessed far greater organization and infiltration into Rhodesia than Nkomo's ZAPU, with its vastly superior weaponry. ZAPU's political decision to hold back the bulk of its forces reinforced the image of ZANLA as the movement truly fighting for the liberation of Zimbabwe.

How was ZANU's nationalism constructed? It fused anticolonialism and twentieth-century ideological thinking and organization with traditional national forces and beliefs, combining ideas of the progressive nation-state with populist African faith systems, social discontent, and national grievances. It drew directly on the role of Shona spirit mediums in the first Chimurenga struggle of the 1890s. This was a tactical maneuver aimed at winning the hearts and minds of the people in eastern Zimbabwe along the Mozambican border. Mugabe himself was later skeptical about spirit mediums. As he told Father Traber in April 1979, "There are just too many *midzimu* . . . far beyond the traditional Shona belief. It is all too much for my liking."[13] This comment reflects Mugabe's Westernized and elitist Zezuru sense of superiority over other Shona-speaking communities. However, with the help of the spirit mediums, ZANLA guerrillas were able to infiltrate areas and politicize the rural population, establish arms caches, and recruit aspiring fighters.

ZANLA recruited from particular Shona-speaking areas in eastern Zimbabwe, and then reentered and dominated the rural population—but crucially, both Zimbabwean radical nationalist movements appealed to and operated in both language groups inside the country. This was a complicated and often ugly picture of peasant mobilization. ZANU used protest literature and particularly music to denounce colonial rule. Popular African protest songs (known as Chimurenga music, with traditional instruments and rhythms) were used by guerrilla fighters in the camps and to mobilize support for the liberation struggle. However, there were also substantial levels of violence to co-opt rural support. Although the use of intimidation, mutilation, mass killings, and rape was officially against party instructions, in the field these tactics were often deployed to brutal effect. Caught between the Rhodesian security forces' increasingly ferocious counterinsurgency campaign and the guerrillas' deliberate use of violence as a political tool, it was the hapless rural population in eastern and southeastern Zimbabwe which bore the brunt.

At the same time there remained a sharp division between the leadership of the political and military wings of the struggle. Conflict arose when Mugabe was thought to be interfering in military matters, and vice versa.[14] Mugabe was relatively overshadowed by ZANLA's veteran military commanders, Nhongo and Tongogara, and only belatedly emerged as the symbol of the movement.[15] Mugabe did not possess a physically commanding presence and relied on his creativity and imagination to instill confidence. His willingness to fight for as long and as hard as was necessary to triumph was another important factor, although Mugabe was patently not a warrior. Instead he presented himself as the eloquent orator, whereas Tongogara was the charismatic, brilliant, but brutal military leader.[16] Mugabe's emergence as ZANU leader was controversial. Some detractors felt that this was a personal "power grab" that betrayed the political principles of their movement.[17]

Faced with internal tensions and factional machinations, Mugabe's heavy-handedness further complicated and exacerbated these strains. "What should have been an exercise in discipline turned into centralization of power" and the brutalization of young fighters.[18] The rebel fighters' grievances mounted against the corruption and elitism of the ZANLA commanders. Ethnic rivalries between the Karanga and Manica further complicated the struggle.

After Geneva, Mugabe lost what little faith he had had in diplomacy and a negotiated settlement. He was quite convinced the conflict could be settled only by "a bitter and bloody war," which could be resolved "only on the battlefield." It proved impossible to persuade him to talk to Ian Smith, and he was implacably insistent on the need for retribution. British foreign secretary David Owen picked up on Mugabe speaking to "a collective brief." However, he impressed Owen with his honesty.[19] Mugabe remained acutely skeptical of continued Anglo-American attempts to broker a settlement, unlike the pragmatist Joshua Nkomo, who was far readier to agree to a solution. Ultimately, though, it was Nkomo who miscalculated in thinking that by not splitting the Patriotic Front he would emerge as its eventual leader.

Between 1977–79 the civil war inside Rhodesia intensified dramatically, as ZANU forces increasingly infiltrated Rhodesia from neighboring Mozambique and the Rhodesian security forces retaliated. Against the escalating violence in the countryside, the Rhodesian Front government embarked on internal negotiations with the moderate nationalists, Bishop Abel Muzorewa, Sithole, and prominent Rhodesian traditional chiefs, leading to an Internal Settlement in March 1978. Owen then began months of clandestine diplomacy to see if the settlement could be widened to include Joshua Nkomo. Both the British and the Rhodesians were determined to exclude Mugabe from any power-sharing agreement. Owen's plans were wrecked by President Nyerere, who denounced Zambia's involvement and deeply embarrassed the Nigerian government, which had tried to help broker a deal.

Against this backdrop of public discord among Africa's leading statesmen, Mugabe remained intent on prosecuting the struggle. His New Year message to the ZANU faithful in 1979, code-named "*Gore reGukurahundi*" (The Year of the People's Storm), was accompanied by a massive recruitment drive and a stepping up of attacks all over the country, with the aim of establishing local committees under the direction of the party. (Groups of ZANLA troops 100 strong infiltrated Rhodesia, and by June there were at least 13,000 ZANLA guerrillas in the country.) The Muzorewa government offered an amnesty in the vain hope that Mugabe's and Nkomo's movements would lay down their arms. As the United Kingdom foresaw, it was only when the Internal Settlement failed to bring peace and stability to the country, with a resulting deadlock in the power struggle, that there would be a greater chance of an internationally negotiated settlement.

The arrival of Mrs. Thatcher in Downing Street in May 1979 proved to be a game changer in the history of the liberation war. Despite a vocal Conservative right wing which regarded Robert Mugabe as the demonic leader of the "pro-Soviet, totalitarian, terrorist Patriotic Front,"[20] Foreign Secretary Lord Carrington (with Thatcher's initially reluctant backing) embarked on one last diplomatic drive to resolve the long-running crisis. The Patriotic Front leaders were deeply angered at their exclusion from the Commonwealth Heads of Government conference in Lusaka in August and the summit's decision to convene an all-party conference in London in September. Having persuaded the head of the Zimbabwe/Rhodesian Government of National Unity, Bishop Muzorewa, to attend, the pressure was now on the liberation leaders to come to the table. Mugabe saw no need to negotiate, convinced that the tide of events was flowing his way: the longer the war lasted, the greater the chances of achieving his ultimate objectives and dictating his terms.[21] Aware of this, the Rhodesian security forces tried to assassinate him twice in Maputo in June 1979.[22] Mugabe only agreed to attend the London talks under intense pressure from southern African leaders at the Non-Aligned Movement meeting in Havana in early September 1979.

Throughout the Lancaster House talks it was deliberate British government policy "to run fast" and to drive the Zimbabwean nationalist negotiators hard.[23] The British were well aware that the unity of the Patriotic Front was largely a fiction.[24] With the painful lesson of the Geneva conference at the forefront of British thinking, a great deal of time and care was devoted to the framing of the all-party talks and the order in which issues where addressed.[25] Carrington's team exploited the "home turf" advantage and excluded the Americans and the Commonwealth as much as possible. Charles Powell was designated as the Foreign Office liaison official with ZANU and tasked with regular private meetings with Mugabe and his colleagues. Powell recalled meeting Mugabe, describing a cold, aloof, and isolated figure, sitting in his coat in a bleak hotel room near Marylebone. Carrington had astutely realized that Mugabe was "the one party who was not particularly enthusiastic about a conference or impatiently in favour of a settlement . . . reckon[ing] the tide of events was anyway flowing his way; that his people would, given time, outlast their enemies . . . that he was comparatively young; that he need assent to nothing unless it provided certainty that he would emerge on top."[26]

These were tense and bitterly controversial negotiations, fraught with brinkmanship and repeated threats of walkouts. In recognition of the political disaster which would ensue if Mugabe were to come to harm in London, Mugabe was protected by a Scotland Yard detail throughout the fifteen-week talks—a wise decision, as the Rhodesian secret service tried to assassinate him during the negotiations.[27] The accommodation of each of the Zimbabwean nationalist delegations was bugged by their British hosts, and summaries of their discussions were relayed to Carrington's team every morning when it would convene to discuss how to handle the day's negotiations. This ensured that the small British team was fully briefed on the thinking of the three Zimbabwean delegations and could tailor British handling of the conference discussions accordingly. Carrington's technique was to hold a series of bilateral meetings with each delegation, to present British proposals for the delegations to consider. Within a short space of time, Carrington would decree that there had been enough opportunity for discussion, and ask for their decision. There was a brutal logic to Carrington's approach, given the backdrop of the ongoing war in Rhodesia and massively destructive Rhodesian army raids in neighboring Zambia and Mozambique.

Mugabe viewed the conference proceedings with enormous distrust, betrayed by his nervous and agitated demeanor on meeting Carrington at the formal opening of the conference. By contrast, Joshua Nkomo made the greater impression as a negotiator and lead spokesperson for the Patriotic Front.[28] Mugabe was consistently quieter, listening carefully and only interjecting after others had declared their position. During each of the three great crises of the conference—over the constitutional proposals for land, the transition arrangements, and the ceasefire proposals the conference came perilously close to breaking up—it was Mugabe who was the most obdurate. It required the diplomatic input of multiple actors to achieve success.

Given the subsequent importance of land in Zimbabwean politics, it is worth considering Mugabe's part in the settlement that emerged at Lancaster House. "Stolen land" had been one of the key "national grievances" behind the liberation struggle, and the rhetoric of liberation fighters had stimulated popular expectations of far-reaching land restitution. Furthermore, since 1977, an international development fund of US$1.2 billion had formed an integral part of the Anglo-American proposals for an internationally recognized settlement. Therefore, although the British negotiators at Lancaster House were at pains to declare that this sum was no longer on the table, it had become embedded in popular nationalist expectations of land transformation and substantial British largesse. The available evidence points to a deliberate policy by Britain to manage a potentially explosive question, rather than an abnegation of responsibility, given the political and regional context of 1979.[29] This contrasted sharply with Mugabe's understandable declaratory stress on British moral responsibility as the formal colonial power. To Mugabe, land was important in terms of redressing the theft by a colonial regime and an element in the future transformation of the country's economy. Land therefore formed part of an agenda of power, as a key element of political mobilization, rather than the driving force to address land hunger.[30]

Mugabe was infuriated by the Muzorewa delegation's refusal to discuss points of difference with the Patriotic Front delegations. Speaking to a British journalist in

1990, he recalled: "At one time I said, 'Oh look here, why even on a fundamental issue like land don't you say something? You see, that was the main grievance throughout the war, land, land, land . . .' [Y]ou are Africans, how dare you accept that the proposition on land shall be governed by the Bill of Rights? We can't get anywhere with the Bill of Rights. Don't you remember your history? The land was never bought from us. Support our position on this one!' They said no, they could not."[31]

The southern African observer group of Botswana, Mozambique, Tanzania, and Zambia held regular sessions with Mugabe and Nkomo. These comprised informal evening meetings at the Commonwealth secretary general's private residence, as well as regular discussions between Commonwealth African high commissioners at Marlborough House, the headquarters of the Commonwealth Secretariat. The message from these meetings was that there was a well-established precedent in how land would be addressed in the constitutional discussions: either by prompt payment of adequate compensation for land or compulsory property purchase by the state. Mugabe was incensed that Zimbabwe was not being treated differently from "any normal country without a land distribution problem." "It must be accepted that full and unfettered political, military and economic power must (be vested) in the people as a whole and that . . . the constitution must contain no racist or other abridgement on the power of the people acting either directly or through their representatives in Parliament to freely alter or abolish it."[32]

As the conference appeared to be breaking down, Mugabe got in touch with Mark Chona, Zambian president Kenneth Kaunda's special political adviser. "[He] called me to his flat and told me the negotiations were going to collapse over land. 'Could you please call your American friends and ask them if Kissinger's pledge [for a development fund] is still on the table?' So I picked up the phone . . . and I called [US diplomat] Gib Lanpher, who was . . . an observer [at Lancaster House]. I asked him a straight question, if that offer was still available, and Gib said, 'Well, Mark, I can't say it is still viable, but we'd be prepared to consider the possibility of funding that kind of programme.'"[33] This, combined with a separate request to the Americans from Ramphal and hurried high-level consultation with the White House, produced an American commitment to help underwrite substantial land restitution.

Throughout the Lancaster House negotiations, the British had signaled "with winks and nods" to General Peter Walls, head of the Rhodesian security forces and a formidable member of Muzorewa's delegation, that Mugabe would be excluded from the final settlement.[34] Mugabe similarly found himself increasingly isolated on the transition arrangements when the proposal was made for a British governor. He described the proposals for the ceasefire at a press conference as "just rubbish. Absolute rubbish."[35] It required President Machel's personal intervention to persuade a bitter Mugabe to sign the Lancaster House settlement.[36] A back-channel appeal from the Foreign Office to President Machel outmaneuvered Mugabe. The message came back from Maputo that there were no issues at stake which would justify the breakup of the conference, and Mozambique was not prepared to accept responsibility for this. The ZANU delegation was informed that they could remain in Mozambique, but "they would be on the beach" writing their memoirs, as no training camps or rear bases would be permitted.

On the face of it Mugabe was the major loser at Lancaster House. He had little to show for his revolutionary rhetoric and repeated attempts to take an independent stand from Nkomo. One-man-one-vote had been watered down to a 20 percent blocking vote for the whites (3 percent of the population); the land deal meant not even uncultivated land could be expropriated without compensation; the new government would inherit both public debt and pensions; and the Rhodesian army would form the core of a new Zimbabwe army, rather than being disbanded. Furthermore, the charismatic army commander Josiah Tongogara appeared to have stolen the diplomatic limelight by being surprisingly conciliatory.[37] Machel's message reached Mugabe as he was on the point of leaving London, following the inconclusive final plenary session at Lancaster House, to take his case to the United Nations in New York. A contemporary photograph of the Patriotic Front leaders shows a furious Mugabe, whose twisted facial features radiate his anger and humiliation that his arguments for escalating to all-out war had been publicly overruled. Mugabe's body language in the surviving news footage betrays his enduring sense of having been cheated: the Lancaster House "deal" had robbed him of victory.[38]

The truth was that by the time of the ceasefire in early January 1980 his military forces had been weakened by Rhodesian attacks.[39] However, now the struggle for Zimbabwe shifted to the ballot box. Mugabe left London without consulting Nkomo on a common approach, and announced at the meeting of southern African leaders in Mozambique that ZANU would be fighting the election as a separate party.[40] Mugabe and his wife returned to Zimbabwe in February 1980 to rapturous crowds. His political manifesto was unexpectedly moderate, singularly lacking Marxist rhetoric or calls for revolutionary transformation. (Machel had strongly advised this approach, but this was largely overlooked by commentators.) The subsequent election campaign was bitter and divisive, with violence and intimidation, and dirty tricks by all three sides. ZANU-PF was the greatest culprit. Over 17,000 fighters arrived at assembly camps, but another 7,000–10,000 political commissars remained in the rural areas to "deliver" the election. Mugabe himself survived two further assassination attempts by Rhodesian security forces.

His relationship with the British governor, Christopher Soames, remained fraught throughout the election campaign.[41] Given proven reports of intimidation, there was considerable pressure on Soames to proscribe Mugabe and his party—from the Rhodesian military, as well as from Muzorewa and Nkomo. Soames realized this would spell disaster: "to disallow Mugabe's involvement would make nonsense of all (the UK) had been trying to achieve, and would place at probably fatal risk the international endorsement . . . so tenuously procured."[42] At the end of February 1980, the election result became clear: ZANU-PF had won 57 seats, Nkomo's party 20, Bishop Abel Muzorewa's party had secured only 3, with the Rhodesian Front sweeping the designated block of 20 white seats. It was the first time an apparently avowed Marxist had been voted into power in Africa. Before the result was announced, the threat of a coup by Rhodesian middle-ranking officers loomed. This was averted only by intense British pressure. Another coup, planned to coincide with Independence Day and backed by the South African military intelligence, was thwarted by the Rhodesian Special Branch.[43]

Despite his sweeping victory, Mugabe's position appeared vulnerable to potential threats—from the South African apartheid government, appalled that the ballot box had delivered victory to a radical black nationalist; and from a deeply angered and resentful Nkomo, who was shattered by the election result and still regarded himself as the rightful father of Zimbabwean nationalism. Mugabe initially tried to persuade Nkomo to accept the ceremonial presidency, but with access to cabinet papers and the brief to advise Mugabe. Nkomo rejected this offer, and when Mugabe's proposal was then leaked, the idea was unanimously vetoed by his ZANU colleagues.[44] It took considerable pressure from President Kaunda and all the persuasive powers of his highly experienced emissary, Mark Chona, to induce Nkomo to join in a government of national unity as minister of home affairs. Nkomo remained profoundly disgruntled, as he did not believe he had been given a suitably important portfolio by Mugabe, whom he regarded as his former junior.

Mugabe came to recognize the enormity of the task he faced in transforming Zimbabwe's war economy, reintegrating the returning fighters and refugees in a hostile regional environment, and facing implacable internal critics and their disgruntled and heavily armed fighters.[45] He came to value Soames and tried to persuade the governor to stay on for eighteen months. Soames's presence would have represented the imprimatur of British support and continued investment in Mugabe's new position. Although Soames refused to stay for more than six weeks, he used his considerable political influence in Whitehall to secure more funds to support Zimbabwe's reconstruction. At Soames's encouragement, Prime Minister Thatcher also wrote to President Carter, who promised to increase dramatically America's support for reconstruction and development. Soames also actively encouraged Mugabe's apparent moderation. In fact, Mugabe surprised everybody.[46]

Ten years before Nelson Mandela's similar gesture of goodwill and policy of reconciliation, Mugabe went on television to declare:

> If yesterday I fought you as an enemy, today you have become a friend and ally in the same national interests, loyalty, rights and duties as myself. If yesterday you hated me, today you cannot avoid the love that binds you to me and me to you. If ever we look to the past, let us do so for the lesson the past has taught us, namely that oppression and racism are iniquities that must never again find scope in our political and social system. It could never be a correct justification that because the whites oppressed us yesterday when they had the power, the blacks must oppress them today because they have the power. An evil remains an evil whether practiced by white against blacks or by black against white.[47]

To the remaining 170,000 Zimbabwean whites, Mugabe's determination "to draw a line through the past" made a remarkable impression.[48] It was also an appeal to Africans who might be contemplating reprisals. How to square this image of a benevolent and forgiving Mugabe with his later antagonism? Carrington summed it up as Mugabe's responding directly to the environment around him: faced with a tense and threatening situation, as in Geneva, he proved vindictive and resentful, swift to condone violence against his opponents. However, flushed with triumph in 1980, he could be generous and magnanimous. Ken Flower, the long-standing director of the Central Intelligence Organisation who served as the first intelligence/security adviser and head of CIO to Mugabe, felt in 1980 the president emerged "as someone with a greater capacity and determination to shape the country's destiny for the benefit of all its people than any of his four predecessors."[49] He was "conciliation personified," his "own man," "careful in his considerations, a fine judge of a man's worth," someone who attached great weight to personal loyalty and felt a corresponding sense of betrayal if this was not publicly and privately consistent.[50]

President Machel, too, had urged him to encourage the whites to stay, and to include Smith in government. At this, Mugabe laughed and murmured, "We will have to think about that." Nyerere did not support this idea of including Ian Smith, but felt that the government should include some whites.[51] As further insurance against Rhodesian military disaffection, Soames also encouraged Mugabe to keep the Rhodesian army commander, General Walls, who was mystified to be told by Mugabe, "The teachings of Karl Marx are identical to those of Jesus Christ." Walls agreed to stay out of a sense of patriotism, only to resign the following year.

It is clear that Mugabe initially made a profound impression on those around him. "It was a time when he really cared about the country. When he really cared about the people."[52] There was considerable relief among remaining white Rhodesians, especially white farmers.

On the advice of Machel and Nyerere, Mugabe accepted the principle of keeping Rhodesian civil servants, with appointed African deputies who would replace them as they retired. There were intense hopes for the future of a prosperous multiracial Zimbabwe, as a showcase for transition for the greater problem of apartheid South Africa. However, to the observant, there were early signs of trouble soon after the 1980 election campaign in the roadblocks manned by white troops between Victoria Falls and Bulawayo.[53] The Zimbabwean security forces feared that returning disaffected ZIPRA fighters, trained by the Cubans in neighboring Angola and armed by the Soviet Union, would be mobilized against their political opponents.

The honeymoon was short lived. To Mugabe, reconciliation meant starting afresh, and forgetting the past. Those who didn't agree would find themselves "in trouble."[54] Mugabe's emphasis on reconciliation was not shared by others within ZANU-PF. The militants wanted to press ahead with the revolutionary transformation of Zimbabwe, even if this offended the whites. More serious was the situation in Matabeleland where ex-ZAPU fighters had buried Soviet-made arms caches.[55] Sporadic fighting and attacks on farmers and civilians broke out in Bulawayo in early 1981. Mugabe was also under pressure from Nkomo to allow the opening of a Soviet embassy in Harare. Given the substantial level of Soviet military support for ZAPU during the liberation struggle, there was a continued fear of the ZAPU/Soviet relationship within the

ZANU-PF leadership.[56] Nkomo's repeated demands for the opening of a Soviet embassy[57] encouraged Mugabe's contact with North Korea in August 1981, and the subsequent military training of the ex-ZANLA Shona-speaking Fifth Brigade, accountable to the prime minister.

Together with the flawed land settlement, this failure to address the issue of rival nationalist armies has later been judged as one of the most serious failures of peacemaking at Lancaster House.[58] In 1979 the Patriotic Front delegations "had hardly any plans about the future of the guerrillas who decided not to join the army."[59] Carrington had only raised this once—that many guerrillas would want to return to civilian life, and this would be the responsibility of the government post independence. However, it was comprehensively overlooked by the Patriotic Front.[60] White Zimbabwean officers were acutely aware of the problems and dangers of fusing two separate guerrilla armies. The British military training team tasked with creating a national army from disciplined troops and poorly trained guerrilla fighters was equally aware of the challenges. As heavily armed ZIPRA fighters established themselves at a strategic redoubt in Matabeleland, local observers and journalists warned that war was looming. Mugabe's argument to camera was calm but uncompromising—as he told Thames *TV Eye* in 1981, "in any event, we will have to disarm them, whether they like it or not."[61]

Mugabe's speech to the Zimbabwe Parliament in April 1981 clearly indicated that ZANU-PF was the only party which should represent Zimbabweans. "The concept of setting up a party merely to oppose . . . and not to assist a government in being, to govern on a national basis, is repugnant to me. Not that I have anti democratic principles, but rather that I cherish the principle of national unity . . . where their main concern is achieving peace, getting people to work together nationally . . . embarking on programmes of development where everybody's effort is required. To my mind, it is a luxury to indulge in the politics of opposition."[62] "We were not fighting [the war] for the two major tribes . . . we were fighting it for one people who are now constituted into one nation, and it is this one-ness that we would want to see urged and facilitated."[63]

This was a clear call for a one-party state. As the North Korean–trained Fifth Brigade moved into Matabeleland to crush the dissidents, British media reports appeared on the atrocities, which were steadfastly denied by Zimbabwe government spokesmen. Political commentators were slow to realize Mugabe's degree of ultimate responsibility. "He was such an articulate person, he was such an intelligent person. To imagine him as a thug? I really could not get that into my head."[64] Western leaders and diplomats were in an acute quandary: the British had 100 officers retraining the new Zimbabwe national army. If this failed, would the country slide into all-out civil war? Mugabe adeptly deflected British journalists' suggestions at press conferences that Amnesty International should be allowed into southern

Zimbabwe to investigate the violence and killings, with a robust countercharge that Britain would never dream of doing this in Northern Ireland during the Troubles. Prime Minister Thatcher had a long and uncomfortable meeting with Mugabe in May 1983 discussing "his increasingly tyrannical imposition of a one-party state, rigged trials for RAF officers (who were Zimbabwe citizens) and rumours of political murders."[65] For the Commonwealth, which had presented itself as the proud midwife of Zimbabwe's independence, it appeared a very confused picture, but the Commonwealth secretary general, Sonny Ramphal, accepted African states' determined attachment to sovereignty and non-interference and failed to act. It was a shameful silence. Nkomo fled from Zimbabwe and appealed to external backers of the Lancaster House settlement, but nothing was done. By 1987, the Fifth Brigade's violence against the Ndebele and Kalanga people had resulted in at least 20,000 deaths and a deeply traumatized community.[66] ZAPU had run out of friends and options. In 1987, ZAPU signed a Unity Pact with ZANU-PF, and Zimbabwe became an effective one-party state under its new president, Robert Mugabe.

4

Refashioning the State, and the Hope of Multiracial Zimbabwe

Mugabe's grip on power after signing the Unity Accord with Nkomo on December 27, 1987, was stronger than ever. In a ceremony just three days later, Parliament declared him executive president, to the refrain of "You Are the Only One."[1] Mugabe now combined the roles of head of state, head of government, and commander in chief of the defense forces. He had powers to dissolve Parliament and declare martial law. His office controlled all the major levers of power, including the civil service, defense force, police, and parastatal organizations. Mugabe's hand was further strengthened by the expiry of the agreement reached at Lancaster House reserving whites 20 seats in the 100-seat lower house of parliament.

As if these powers were insufficient, the state of emergency that Ian Smith had introduced was retained. It was finally lifted in 1990, but even then the president held many arbitrary powers of detention. State radio and television were also tightly controlled by the government, with only a handful of independent newspapers attempting to provide an alternative to the official sycophantic coverage of Mugabe and his government. The leading independent newspapers were the *Daily News* and three weekly publications: the *Financial Gazette, Zimbabwe Independent,* and *Sunday Standard.* Newspaper editors and journalists were routinely put under pressure, with arrests and attacks on their offices. Press restrictions tightened just as middle-class urban opposition grew. The *Daily News* was critically important, with a readership of around 900,000, and came under intense pressure.[2] Its printing press was bombed in 2002 and it was shut down the following year after it refused to register under the government's draconian legislation.

Mugabe was also leader of ZANU-PF. Although on the face of it Joshua Nkomo and ZAPU were brought into the fold, they had little say in the direction of the party. Mugabe had subordinated his main political rival as nationalist leader. The ZANU-PF Politburo and Central Committee became the main focus of political debate, usurping the policy-making roles of the cabinet and of Parliament itself. This included the establishment of a Politburo committee to supervise the work of civil servants, leading to a public dispute with the minister responsible for the civil service, Eddison Zvobgo.[3] Soon the civil service was populated with party loyalists, whose chief remit was to satisfy their political masters.

Senior politicians began using their newfound resources to purchase property. By 1990 senior party leaders, including the two vice presidents and the president's sister, had all acquired farms.[4] At a local level, ZANU-PF mayors and town councilors followed suit. The *Economist* concluded that looting of the parastatals and corruption in the public sector had reached "epidemic" proportions.[5]

As has been indicated earlier, land was the key issue in the newly liberated country. Dispossession had been a critical problem since the 1830s, when the Ndebele invaded from South Africa, fleeing from the Zulu revolution, known as the *mfecane*. The Ndebele had lost many of their own people during this migration and engaged in what Professor Sabelo Ndlovo-Gatsheni describes as "limited wars of conquest of the south-west since the people of this area did not readily accept their rule."[6] Seizing territory in what is today Zimbabwe from tribes that became known as the Shona, the Ndebele made their home in the west of the country, around Bulawayo.[7] The Pioneer Column sent by Cecil Rhodes in 1890 marked the beginning of an even more extensive dispossession.[8] Vast tracts of land were taken and distributed by Rhodes's British South Africa Company to the white "pioneers" who had served its aim of securing mineral rights. Rhodes had promised each of the 200 pioneers free farms of 3,175 acres. But men like Major Sir John Willoughby, formerly of the Royal Horse Guards and chief of staff of the Pioneer Column, were given far larger land holdings.[9] He alone was granted a staggering 600,000 acres. Willoughby went on to buy further stretches of land as whites moved off farms to seek their fortunes on the mines, eventually accumulating no less than 1.3 million acres. Missionaries too were granted large tracts of land. Within ten years of the arrival of the pioneers the whites had taken nearly sixteen million acres—or one-sixth of the entire land mass of the country. This deprivation of their land (predominantly in the more fertile and less disease-prone areas of the country, with higher rainfall) was fiercely resisted by the black population, who rose twice in the period 1896–97. First the Ndebele and then the Shona fought back in what became known as the Chimurenga.

Over the next century this annexation continued, and by independence in 1980 just 6,000 large-scale, mostly white, farmers owned 42 percent of all the land.[10] These commercial farmers, well capitalized and using modern farming techniques, dominated the agricultural sector. They were successful, producing three-quarters of all output and 95 percent of all sales. By contrast, approximately 4 million black Africans were making a living in the overcrowded communal lands, comprising 41 percent of the country. There they grew crops for consumption rather than for export.[11] A government commission established after independence recommended that nearly half of the black farmers should be resettled. The commission concluded that the communal areas could only sustain 325,000 of the 780,000 families who lived on them; the remainder would have to be found new farms.[12] Somehow this land would have to be acquired, if the war against white rule was to have any meaning.

During the first ten years of independence the land redistribution program had to operate under the terms of the Lancaster House agreement.[13] As has been seen, when the issue was being debated in London, Mugabe had denounced other African leaders for not taking a harder stand on this issue.[14] In the end a compromise was arrived at. Compulsory land acquisition had to take place on a "willing seller, willing buyer" basis and in 1981 the British government provided £20 million to fund the program.[15] There was also a very substantial multilateral aid agreement, which included development of the rural economy, although the Canadians were the only other foreign government expressly to earmark aid for land reform. The land was purchased from the mainly white farmers represented by the Commercial Farmers Union, who had produced the majority of the agricultural output that fed the towns and went for export. The process was slow and cumbersome, exacerbated by the fact that the injection of demand inflated land prices. The government also had too few civil servants competent to implement the program.[16] By 1990 only modest progress had been made in achieving a real transfer of land to the majority population.

One of the issues that brought matters to a head was the growing realization that many choice farms were being acquired by the elite who surrounded Mugabe. "By 1990 a new class of landowners was firmly established:

ministers, MPs, senior civil servants, police and defence officials, and parastatal managers. In all, they had managed to acquire 8 percent of commercial farmland since independence, although little of it was put to productive use."[17] Not all the money Britain had provided to help purchase farms had been taken up by the Zimbabwean authorities. The British overseas development minister pointed this out to the Mugabe government in 1988, but received no reply.[18] Tensions with Britain rose and were exacerbated when the Labour aid minister, Clare Short, wrote to Mugabe in November 1997 suggesting that her Irish ancestry meant that she too was a victim of British history and therefore could not be held responsible for previous British imperialism.[19] "I should make it clear that we do not accept that Britain has a special responsibility to meet the costs of land purchase in Zimbabwe. We are a new government from diverse backgrounds without links to former colonial interests. My own origins are Irish and as you know we were colonised and not colonisers." Mugabe saw the remarks as incendiary. Furious, he described Prime Minister Tony Blair as "worse than the Tories."[20]

While relations with Britain were deteriorating, Zimbabwe was forging new ties with its neighbors. Mugabe's relationship with South Africa's ruling party after 1994—and Nelson Mandela's presidency—was particularly important. Liberation movements led both nations after 1994. On the face of it they should have had much in common. In reality the relations were fraught—dating back to the struggles against white rule. Mugabe's party ZANU had been aligned with the Chinese and at least nominally in alliance with South Africa's second-largest liberation movement, the Pan Africanist Congress. It was Joshua Nkomo's ZAPU that had strong ties with the ANC leadership and their supporters in the Soviet Union.[21]

The ANC established a military alliance with Nkomo on August 15, 1967.[22] The deal was signed as ANC cadres were deployed alongside ZAPU guerrillas who fought a series of bloody but not particularly successful battles against the Rhodesian armed forces, in what became known as the Wankie campaign of August and September of that year. As a result, South African paramilitary police units were sent into the Zambezi valley, while South African communication engineers established a permanent listening post next to Lake Kariba. The action was sharply criticized by Mugabe's South African allies—the Pan Africanist Congress. They argued that it was a mistake to take on a regular army in a conventional battle; what was needed was guerrilla warfare. ZANU's official newspaper *Zimbabwe News* took a similar line. If the ANC wished to help Zimbabweans, they should fight in South Africa, not in Rhodesia.[23]

When the results of Zimbabwe's first election were announced at the London headquarters of the Anti-Apartheid Movement (which took its lead from the ANC) there were very long faces indeed when Robert Mugabe emerged as the victor. The South African Communist Party (allies of the ANC) at first regarded

ZANU's victory as the result of a "conspiracy with international capital"[24]—which was ironic, since Mugabe was a self-proclaimed Marxist. Cold War allegiances in Southern Africa were notoriously complicated. Reestablishing trust between the ANC and ZANU took a long time. The Mandela presidency had relatively little to do with Mugabe. It was left to Thabo Mbeki (who had played a key role in ANC foreign policy for years and took over the reins of power in June 1999) to attempt to deal with Zimbabwe's growing malaise. Thabo Mbeki went out of his way to accommodate Mugabe. As Mbeki's biographer Mark Gevisser described, their relationship was built on a shared belief that they faced a white enemy, both in South Africa and in the West. As black Africans they were "kith and kin," and Mbeki would not allow them to be divided.[25] Rather, using the mandate given him by regional leaders in the Southern African Development Community (SADC), he attempted to achieve a mediated resolution to Zimbabwe's political crises.

The Mbeki government did everything in its power not to put pressure on its northern neighbor, despite intense demands from the international community. Quite why this was the case has been a matter of speculation for some time. The academic Merle Lipton explained this (at least in part) by South Africa's reluctance to abrogate the principle of sovereignty and noninterference in the affairs of another state—especially one led by another national liberation movement.[26] But she acknowledged that Pretoria's position was "perplexing." While she provides some possible explanations, they are tentative at best.

Mbeki himself has recently offered his own interpretation of why he was so determined to stand by Robert Mugabe. It was—he says—an attempt to head off regime change.[27] "In the period preceding the 2002 Zimbabwe Elections, the UK and the US in particular were very keen to effect this regime change and failing which to impose various conditions to shorten the period of any Mugabe Presidency. Our then Minister of Intelligence, Lindiwe Sisulu, had to make a number of trips to London and Washington to engage the UK and US governments on their plans for Zimbabwe, with strict instructions from our Government to resist all plans to impose anything on the people of Zimbabwe, including by military means." Mbeki went on to cite Lord Guthrie, former chief of defense staff of the UK armed forces, as saying, "Astonishingly, the subjects discussed" with Prime Minister Tony Blair included invading Zimbabwe, "which people were always trying to get me [Guthrie] to look at. My advice was, 'Hold hard, you'll make it worse.'"

It is difficult to know what to make of this story. A spokesman for the former British prime minister denied the allegations: "Tony Blair has long believed that Zimbabwe would be much better off without Robert Mugabe and always argued for a tougher stance against him, but he never asked anyone to plan or take part in any such military intervention."[28] In reality it need never have come to this. One of Mbeki's white predecessors, John Vorster, had merely turned the screws on the Rhodesian regime: slowing imports and leaving the country short of oil and other vital supplies for the government to cave in; but this was a path Mbeki was not prepared to contemplate.[29]

Certainly, South Africa would have never accepted that an outside power (especially a former imperial power like Britain) should oust a neighbor. But the relationship is more complex than that. There was also an element of indebtedness: Zimbabwe had put its land reform program on hold in 1990–93 because of negotiations on South Africa's transition, and to reassure white South Africans.[30] Stephen Chan, a longtime Zimbabwe analyst, puts it down to a range of reasons.[31] These include a shared intellectual position, an unwillingness to go out on a limb, and Mbeki's assessment that there was really no other suitable leader in Zimbabwe. Perhaps Chan comes closest to explaining the phenomenon when he says: "Mugabe genuinely holds Mbeki, and many other African presidents, in thrall. His personal charisma and position as the grand old man of liberation gives him both seniority and pedigree that no one else can match. What is taken as senseless rhetoric in the West is a rhetoric of great meaning in a continent where the welts and scars of racism and colonialism will take another generation to heal."

There was also an enduring conviction that regime change would be "counterrevolutionary" and regressive, allowing "neoimperialist forces" and their stooges back into southern Africa. This perception played an important part in the mind-set of Marxists and African nationalists. Mbeki was also in an invidious position. He was expected to be the regional "fixer" by the Western powers, yet was looked to by other African governments and leaders to be their champion beyond the African continent. Mbeki adopted a practice of "quiet diplomacy," which put minimum public pressure on Zimbabwe and eschewed the practice of the apartheid government of interfering in its neighbor's affairs. When the Commonwealth moved to suspend Zimbabwe following the contested elections of 2002, Mbeki was a key member of the three-leader "troika" which tried to bring Mugabe back into line on Commonwealth democratic values. This failed miserably at the Abuja meeting in 2003. Mugabe was so furious at what he saw as unacceptable interference in Zimbabwe's sovereignty that he declared Zimbabwe was immediately leaving the Commonwealth without even consulting his ZANU-PF colleagues.[32]

Mbeki was prepared to go to extraordinary lengths to conceal the extent of human rights abuses in Zimbabwe. The South African presidency, from Mbeki to Zuma, spent years fighting court cases to prevent an official report on Zimbabwe's violent 2002 election from being made public.[33] The report had been commissioned by Mbeki from two highly respected South African judges. When it was finally published in 2014, the report was damning. The judges found that the 107 politically motivated murders were what they called the "hallmark" of the election campaign, and that ZANU-PF militia deployed during the process were the "primary perpetrators of the violence." As Justices Dikgang Moseneke and Sisi Khampepe concluded: "Having regard to all the circumstances, and in particular the cumulative substantial departures from international standards of free and fair elections found in Zimbabwe during the pre-election period, these elections, in our view, cannot be considered free and fair."[34] Revealed twelve years after the results were announced, this judgment had only a limited impact.

While South African leaders deferred to Mugabe, another foreign question was making itself felt: the war in the Congo. The Democratic Republic of Congo had been unstable since independence in 1960 when the first prime minister, Patrice Lumumba, was overthrown and then assassinated with the assistance of the Belgians, the CIA, and the British.[35] Having overthrown Lumumba, his successor, Joseph Mobutu, was then ousted by rebels led by Laurent-Désiré Kabila in 1997. But Kabila then fell out with his own former allies, Uganda and Rwanda, which sent forces to attack President Kabila in the capital, Kinshasa.[36] This attack outraged other regional powers. In 1998 Angola, Zimbabwe, and Namibia entered the conflict on the side of the government, in what became known as the Great War of Africa. The fighting was to last for nearly five years, causing the death of over two million people and massive internal displacement. The war ended only in July 2003. Nations as remote as Sudan, Chad, and Eritrea became entangled in the war, but it is Zimbabwe's role that is significant here.

Mugabe's reasons for entering the war were complex, but he was influenced by the fact that he had a substantial military at his disposal and was responding to a request from the Congolese government for forces to ward off "imperialism."[37] The initial deployment of just 600 Zimbabwean troops grew inexorably to 16,000 within thirty months. Whatever the rights or wrongs of this venture, it took an extraordinarily high toll on Zimbabwe. The cost (estimated at US$30 million a month) was admitted by the government to be Z$10 billion in August 2000, and rising.[38] The burden on the Zimbabwean economy was unsustainable, Dr. Simba Makoni, Zimbabwe's finance minister, admitted, but this was not an argument Mugabe was willing to tolerate. "Don't talk of resources as if resources are more important than the security of the people and the sovereignty of the country.... The only way to bring peace to the country is to confront the rebels."[39]

Economist John Robertson put the total cost of the Congo war to Zimbabwe at US$1 billion. The exact number of Zimbabwean lives lost has remained a state secret.[40] There was also a heavy loss of military equipment, which the country could not afford to replace. "On balance," concluded Martin Rupiya, "the country appears to have made a huge sacrifice for its involvement in the war, which has left it scarred, impoverished, and politically divided."[41] The only winners appeared to be the senior officers and businessmen, who were reported to have made vast sums of money out of Congolese diamonds and timber, as well as air cargo and road haulage contracts.[42]

While this foreign engagement was under way, relations between the government and civil society were declining. Three parallel trends developed. The first was the emergence of discontent among the urban working class and the trade union movement; this was a direct product of the failed structural adjustment program of the early 1990s, originally designed to kick-start the Zimbabwean economy. However, state retrenchment directly affected the most vocal section of the population. This found expression in the formation in 1999 of the Movement for Democratic Change (MDC) led by the secretary-general of the Zimbabwe Congress of Trade Unions, Morgan Tsvangirai. The second trend was the gradual erosion of support for the state among the churches. Finally, there was the growing resistance by civil society groups to the attempts by the Mugabe government to reduce their room for maneuver and centralize all power in the hands of the ruling party.

Declining living standards, increases in taxation, and falling health and educational provision led the unions to call a successful "stay-away" in December 1997.[43] In January and February the following year there were food riots in the townships or "high-density areas" around Harare. The protests were first banned, and then the army was sent in to quell the unrest. Tsvangirai was attacked, and the union offices in Bulawayo were burnt down. Despite this the protests continued, both against rising prices and the army's role in the Congo.

The churches, some of which had played key roles in supporting the resistance to white rule, were initially cautious about their relationship with the Mugabe government. While they engaged in criticism of proposals to establish a one-party state in the late 1980s, they were keen not to break their links with the new government.[44] For example, the Catholic Church refused to make public a highly critical report on the atrocities in Matabeleland, leading to the resignation of the respected head of the Catholic Commission for Justice and Peace, Mike Auret. But as time went by the churches' attitude changed. In the late 1990s these concerns crystallized around the constitution. In May 1997 members of the Zimbabwe Council of Churches brought together unions, NGOs, and church members to consider the excessive powers invested in the president and how the constitution might be revised. A National Constitutional Assembly was launched, chaired by Morgan Tsvangirai.

The government's response was perhaps predictable. They launched a rival Constitutional Commission and traveled the country collecting views from ordinary people. Some church leaders were persuaded to participate in this official review, which asked questions such as: "How many terms can the head of state serve?"[45] In the end the Commission's findings were referred to the ruling party, which overruled a number of its recommendations. Some church leaders, including Bishop Ambrose Moyo of the Evangelical Lutheran Church, resigned. A referendum on the proposals from the Commission was scheduled to be put to the people in February 2000. Opponents of the Commission's draft constitution argued that the proposal for an executive presidency would leave too much power in Mugabe's hands, and suggested that executive authority should be replaced with a prime minister accountable to Parliament. Government propaganda accused unnamed and interfering foreign governments and meddling overseas donors of calling for a vote against the new constitution. It was against this background that the Movement for Democratic Change was launched in September 1999, headed by Tsvangirai. With union support, it appeared to be a viable alternative to ZANU-PF. It also had the backing of academics, business leaders, and NGO activists. As such it was—in the view of Sarah Rich Dorman—the "first nationally grounded opposition party to challenge ZANU (PF)."[46]

Mugabe's response was to label his critics "Western stooges." The president and his party declared that rejecting the draft constitution would be tantamount to voting for colonialism. A full-page advertisement in the *Herald,* the main government-run newspaper, showed a white couple wearing Vote No T-shirts above the words: "Don't follow them back to the dark days of the past, when they were kings and queens."[47]

It was against this background that the referendum was held on February 12–13, 2000. To the astonishment of Mugabe and the ruling party, the people voted overwhelmingly against the constitutional proposals, rejecting them by 57.7 percent to 45.3 percent. Crowds celebrated in Harare, waving posters saying "Yellow card Mugabe" and "Tanaura Jongwe," literally "we've plucked the feathers of the cockerel"—the cockerel being the symbol of ZANU-PF, and therefore of Robert Mugabe.[48] Although the president went on television accepting the outcome, he was shaken to the core. Never had he faced a rejection by the people of Zimbabwe. It rocked the legitimacy of his party's rule, and the model of governance he had constructed as leader. In his view, it appeared to threaten letting in "counterrevolutionary" forces; Mugabe was determined it never be repeated.

5

Revolution Redux, or
"Why It All Turned Sour"

The result of the referendum was a devastating blow for Mugabe and taught him a lesson he would never forget. From that moment on he was determined never again to put his trust in his own people: to allow a free and fair vote whose outcome he could not control. Mugabe, who had spent so many years in jail as a national liberation activist, believed it was illegitimate to question the direction that he, their leader, was taking them in. The explanation that presented itself was that national liberation had faltered, and that it risked going into reverse under the pressure of malign external forces. He declared openly that the referendum result had only been brought about by the forces of imperialism.[1] Britain and America, he declared, were working through white farmers and their black surrogates (the farmworkers), who had misled the people of Zimbabwe. Those who supported his opponents were divisive, and "sell-outs."

There were other pressures on the president: there was growing unrest. "By the end of the first structural adjustment programme in 1996, national politics had come to a boil, and the legitimacy of the ruling party as the 'guardian' of the nation was under severe challenge."[2] Beset by rising militancy across the public sector and wildcat strikes by farmworkers, Mugabe's government was also challenged internally by the re-emergence of the war veterans in national politics. Precipitated by a financial scandal and the collapse of the state-sponsored War Veterans Compensation Fund, the war veterans demanded that the state compensate them from the national budget. This opened up the split within the ZANU-PF movement between the elites and their proclaimed policy of "indigenization" and the lower echelons who had missed out on the benefits of independence, many of whom were living in acute poverty. This reignited discontent over the fate of national liberation. Mugabe caved in to the veterans' demands for a substantial compensation package, even though it had not been included in the national budget. In addition, the ZANU-PF government gazetted 1,470 white commercial farms for compulsory acquisition, and promised 20 percent of the farms to the war veterans. Mugabe's policy decisions immediately put enormous pressure on the economy, and the Zimbabwe dollar plummeted. To outsiders they appeared to be entirely self-serving actions by the president. However, "the war veteran challenge was of a different magnitude, for the war vets were also firmly embedded in the state apparatus and, indeed, were in charge of security, including the President's office."[3]

As the Zimbabwe economy spiraled downward, these events galvanized another round of negotiations with international donors leading to a nominal settlement in 1998. However, no progress was made within the country on the land question, and by 2000 national politics was boiling over.

Once Mugabe recovered from the humiliation of the referendum he set about systematically attacking the sources of opposition. He began with the white farmers and their farm workers. Mugabe believed that many of these employees had voted "no" on the instructions of their employers, although there is no evidence for this. The attacks on the farms were followed by an assault on the urban areas that had also rejected ZANU-PF's advice to support the constitutional changes. The next targets were the churches and nongovernmental organizations that backed the opposition. Finally, Mugabe's wrath fell on the opposition parties themselves and the men who led them. This was a lengthy, vicious and well-coordinated campaign to ensure that there would be no chance of removing Mugabe or his party from power, as long as he lived.

Mugabe decided to ride the tiger of land hunger and farm invasions, thereby rekindling ZANU-PF's alliance with peasants and war veterans. In one sense, it could be seen as resistance to "exhausted neo-liberalism" of the 1990s.[4] National grievances over the slow pace of reform and failure to deliver the benefits of liberation were very real across rural Zimbabwe. There had been sporadic farm invasions by nominal "war veterans" (some of whom had never fought in the war of independence) and landless peasants since the mid-1990s. By the late 1990s the government had developed a policy strategy for managed accelerated transition. Thanks to Mugabe, this went by the board, as he unleashed an onslaught on the commercial farmers. Going on television on February 12 as the referendum ended, Mugabe had singled out the white community, declaring that whites had "sloughed off apathy and participated vigorously in the poll." Michael Auret, of the Catholic Church, pointed out that few whites understood just how chilling these words really were.[5] Less than two weeks later, gangs of "war veterans" armed with axes and machetes invaded farms across the country.[6] Transported by government trucks and given rations, they were paid a daily allowance to stake claims to the land. Most were urban unemployed youths who were too young to have fought for their country's independence, but they were described as "war vets" nonetheless. Some of the white farmers whose land was seized had purchased their farms after independence and had certificates to prove that the government had no interest in their property. Despite this, they were taken, often with considerable violence. In July 2000 the dispossession was given a name: the Fast Track Land Reform and Resettlement Programme.

Over the next two years 6 million hectares were confiscated from farmers, most of whom were white. They were redistributed to 127,000 families as small farms and to 7,200 black commercial farmers. But the best land—often close to the major urban areas—went to Mugabe's cronies.[7] This was, argued the South African journalist Alistair Sparks, a pattern that had been established early in the Mugabe presidency. "Eighteen months after independence the Mugabe government had bought up 435,000 acres of white farmland, but resettled fewer than 3,000 black peasants. In a pattern that was to become even more apparent in the years that followed, scores of government-owned farms were being handed out on leases to cabinet ministers, MPs, top civil servants and other senior members of the ruling party—few of which were put to productive use."[8] Some have challenged this view, pointing out that only around 10 percent of the land went to the political elite.[9]

While the experience of black dispossessed farmers failed to make the international headlines, the plight of the white farmers was shown on television across the world. Armed gangs were seen arriving at farmsteads, confronting the owners and then brutally assaulting them if they resisted before looting the home and then putting it to the torch. Dramatic as these images were, they failed to capture the fate of those worst affected by the program: the 1.3–1.9 million farm workers and their families.[10] This radically changed the Zimbabwean rural economy in terms of housing, access to health clinics and education, as well as the farmworkers' future livelihoods. Few understood why they were so badly treated. One farmworker described how her house was burnt down and she was assaulted because she had allegedly supported the opposition: "We were just accused of voting for MDC, quite a number of us were beaten up at the farm, the five of us. I do not even know where the MDC meetings were held."[11] Often their children were forced to watch the beatings, while the victims had to sing liberation songs, or join the ruling party.

Agricultural output plunged. Production of maize, the country's staple crop, was severely reduced, as small-scale farmers struggled with shortages of farm machinery, access to fertilizer and seed, capital to support irrigation infrastructure, and market access. During the years following the 2000 land redistribution, output fell by between a tenth and three-quarters.[12]

Table 1: Zimbabwean annual maize production

Time span 1990s average	2002/3	2005/6	2006/7	2007/8	2009/10	2010/11
Production (000 tonnes)						
1,685.6	1,058.8	1,484.8	952.6	575.0	1,322.66	1,451.6
% change						
	−37.2	−11.9	−43.5	−74.2	−21.5	−13.9

In recent years this trend has continued, exacerbated by severe drought. The UN's Food and Agricultural Organisation (FAO) reported that the 2015 maize harvest was 742 thousand tonnes and that the prospect for 2016 (given the severe drought across the whole of the region) was even worse.[13]

This is an intensely political issue, and others paint a rather different picture. The Zimbabwe government statistical office questioned the totals reported by the FAO and scholars. In 2015, according to the Zimbabwe National Statistics Agency, more than a million tonnes of maize were produced (1.081 million tonnes).[14] Of this total the majority (663,000 tonnes) came from the communal areas—the traditional "African Reserves," as they used to be known. Much of this harvest would traditionally have been consumed by the farmers and their families, not sold on the open market. It is unlikely to have been available to feed the urban population or for export.

A considerable body of literature has emerged calling for a reexamination of the question of land and agriculture.[15] Ian Scoones and his colleagues have produced an alternative interpretation of the program, and they are certainly right in concluding that it is a complex question.[16] They show that the land reform program was not a complete failure and argue that the revolutionary transformation of land access, production, and management would take time to work through; that the beneficiaries were not largely Mugabe's political "cronies"; and that the new settlers did indeed invest in the land that they received. They point out that the rural economy has not collapsed and agriculture is not "in complete ruins creating chronic food insecurity." The authors are correct to indicate that the terrible droughts that have hit the country in recent years were the fault of neither the government nor the new farmers. At the same time, Scoones and his coauthors cannot deny two key points. First, that Zimbabwe has ceased to be a net food exporter and is now almost always a large food-importing nation, one that cannot feed its urban population. Second, that although about 1 million people received farms,[17] approximately as many farmworkers were driven off the land and ended up impoverished in the communal areas, scraping an existence in marginal, highly insecure environments; moving to towns; or going into exile in South Africa.

The results of President Mugabe's land policies are mixed, to say the least. Even those who received farms complain that they have seen few benefits. "We thought when we were placed there that we'd be helped, but no, we were just left," said Alec Kaitano, a twenty-three-year-old who abandoned his smallholding outside the northeastern town of Bindura a year ago and survives by selling blemished fruit he finds in garbage cans in Harare.[18] "Those white farmers we displaced had money to farm, but we didn't, so we failed." There are reports that farms that once grew some of the best tobacco in the world now stand idle and abandoned as farmers head for the urban areas.

While the land was being redistributed there were equally dramatic events in the cities. Mugabe understood the threat that the MDC represented, and he ensured that the party came under sustained attack. As has been seen, particularly in the run-up to the 2000 and 2002 elections, opposition supporters were beaten and MDC rallies broken up. Young ZANU-PF activists, known as the "Green Bombers" and trained in National Service camps, manned roadblocks and attacked MDC members. Polling agents and candidates were kidnapped and "disappeared." Despite these tactics, the MDC did manage to win council elections in the capital in 2002. An MDC mayor and council were elected in the capital in a landslide—with the party taking 44 of the 45 wards in Harare. The mayor, Elias Mudzuri, took over 80 percent of the vote, but the party's victory was not to last. Within a year the mayor had been forced out of office to be replaced by a government-appointed commission.[19]

Aware that the urban populations were no longer reliable, Mugabe moved against them. In October 2004—amid suggestions in the papers that Harare needed "tidying up"—Operation Murambatsvina was launched. It meant, literally, "Drive out rubbish." Systematic urban clearances were undertaken, with shanties demolished, informal markets and workshops shut down, and goods confiscated. The United Nations sent a team to report on what had taken place, led by a Tanzanian, Anna Tibaijuka, executive director of the United Nations Human Settlements Programme.[20] She reported that there had been a systematic destruction of property and livelihoods, carried out by the police and army. "It is estimated that some 700,000 people in cities across the country have lost either their homes, their source of livelihood or both. Indirectly, a further 2.4 million people have been affected in varying degrees," she concluded. "Hundreds of thousands of women, men and children were made homeless, without access to food, water and sanitation, or health care." With their urban base disrupted, the prospects for the opposition were poor. Then they suffered another, self-inflicted, blow. In 2005 the MDC split.[21] One faction was led by Tsvangirai, the other by his former allies, Welshman Ncube and Arthur Mutambara.

The battle to control Zimbabwe's urban population took place as hundreds of thousands of impoverished men and women left for South Africa, believing there was little hope of making a living on the land or in the cities. Working in South Africa was a tradition going back to the nineteenth century, with Zimbabweans traveling to the mines. The liberation war of the 1970s and '80s led to a flight to safety. But it was really only in the 1990s that this trend intensified, with clashes between Mugabe and Nkomo and the wider political unrest. By 1995 over 700,000 Zimbabweans had gone south in search of sanctuary and employment.[22]

As the repression intensified, they were joined by tens of thousands of others. Some were farmworkers who had been displaced by land reform, others came from towns and cities. Most were black, but they were joined by a substantial proportion of Zimbabwe's white population. There was a huge "brain drain," which soon included half of all doctors. By 2009 nearly 150,000 had been granted asylum, but this was a tiny fraction of the Zimbabweans who went to live in South Africa, estimated at between 1.5 million and 3 million.[23] More than half said they still wanted to return to their own country. In the meantime, they were saving the wages and salaries they earned to send goods and money home. As Zimbabwe's economic situation deteriorated, these remittances became increasingly vital for the survival of their families.

By 2008 Zimbabwe was in a sorry state. The formal economy was in sharp decline, harvests had fallen, the opposition supporters in the urban areas had been attacked, and civil society was struggling to survive. Radio stations critical of the government had been closed and opponents physically attacked and intimidated. The chronic instability of the late 1990s, compounded by the chaos and disruption of the revolutionary land program, capital flight and skills emigration, and fiscal mismanagement by the Central Bank, all pulverized the value of the Zimbabwe dollar. In 2008, hyperinflation hit 79.6 billion percent. At that point, the government gave up trying to produce official statistics. Yet worse was to follow.

"Look East" for Foreign Friends

The political crisis came to a head in 2008. General elections were held in March and June of that year, and for a moment it appeared as if the opposition had made a breakthrough. In March the MDC-T won more seats than ZANU-PF (99 to 97). More worrying for Mugabe, he received a lower share of the vote than Tsvangirai (48 percent to 43 percent).[1] The two men had to stand against each other in a runoff election, scheduled for June 27, 2008. The president's response was to unleash a brutal campaign of intimidation, code-named Operation Mavhotera Papi, or "How did you vote?" This was particularly targeted at key opposition strongholds in Mashonaland-East and Midlands. A ZANU-PF Politburo member left the public in no doubt about what was expected of them. "We're giving the people of Zimbabwe another chance to mend their ways, to vote properly . . . this is their last chance." Grace Mugabe, the president's wife, underlined the message. "Even if people vote for MDC, Morgan Tsvangirai will never step foot in State House."[2] Faced with this regime-sanctioned onslaught, which saw murders and kidnapping, vicious beatings, and fire-bombings, Morgan Tsvangirai declared he could not in all conscience ask the Zimbabwean people to vote, and pulled out of the election five days before the poll. In the June election 85 percent backed Mugabe. This terrible period in Zimbabwe's recent history now has a label: "the Fear."

Robert Mugabe had, once again, asserted his authority, but the question of who would rule the country was not resolved. Even if the political crisis had ebbed, the economic crisis had not. Despite his nominal triumph at home, Mugabe found himself under sustained pressure. At an African Union summit he discovered that former allies, including Nigeria, Botswana, Kenya, Liberia, and Senegal gave him a hostile reception.[3] Led by Thabo Mbeki, the region's leaders in the South African Development Community twisted the arms of the main players. Mbeki himself had little time for Morgan Tsvangirai: he did not regard Tsvangirai as a capable leader-in-waiting and he had scant respect for Tsvangirai's limited educational achievements. Furthermore, he came from the trade union movement and was not a liberation leader.[4] Mbeki also had a considerably more powerful union movement of his own—COSATU—and he did not want South African trade unionists to think they could found a party to rival the ANC.

So it was, on July 21, 2008, that the three party leaders—Mugabe and the two leaders of the MDC factions, Tsvangirai and Mutambara—signed a Memorandum of Understanding establishing an inclusive government in which all had a role. The deal, which became known as the Global Political Agreement, overseen by Mbeki, was designed to share power. Yet despite the handshakes, there was little love lost between the political leaders.

If Mugabe was having difficulty making African leaders see things his way and facing opposition from Western capitals, he did not appear particularly disturbed. At home the security forces and the military were clearly supportive of their president, as were key sections of the intelligence services. Abroad Mugabe knew he could rely on other friends: the president turned to the East.

This was, of course, not the first time he had done this. Mugabe's ties with the Chinese went back to the earliest days of his fight with the white rulers of Rhodesia.[5] In 1966 Josiah Tongogara and Emmerson Mnangagwa had been among a group of fighters who were trained at the Nanking Academy. They were taught everything from military intelligence to guerrilla warfare.[6] ZANU's ties were with Beijing, rather than Moscow, which saw ZAPU as its candidate for liberation movement. After independence in 1980, relations between China and Zimbabwe developed gradually, with the construction of hospitals and the National Sports Stadium. Ties were cemented when Mugabe traveled to Beijing in 1985 and returned with loans worth $55 million.[7] When Mugabe decided to eliminate ZAPU as a serious rival, it was to North Korea that he looked, signing a deal with Kim Il Sung in October 1980—an agreement that later led to the formation of the notorious Fifth Brigade, whose murderous activities left thousands dead in Matabeleland.[8] While Western nations might raise troublesome human rights issues, friends in the East did not. As relations with the West deteriorated, Zimbabwe adopted a formal "Look East" policy in 2003, which developed into a "special relationship" with China.[9] "We have turned East, where the sun rises, and given our backs to the West, where the sun sets," Mugabe memorably declared.

The policy soon paid dividends. Not only were there several bilateral meetings, but Beijing was willing to deploy its diplomatic muscle on Zimbabwe's behalf. The Chinese used their veto in the UN Security Council to block sanctions and attempted to intervene directly in the controversial 2008 elections. Beijing's stand contrasted with the European Union's approach. Since 2002 the former president and his wife have faced an EU travel ban and an asset freeze, while the country has been placed under an arms embargo.[10] Beijing stepped in once again. A shipment of Chinese weapons, destined for Zimbabwe, was held up in the South African port of Durban only because trade unionists refused to unload it, following fears that the weapons would be used to repress Mugabe's political rivals.[11] It was a rare example of an international intervention by a nonstate actor to prevent an abuse of human rights, and helped prevent a brutal election from becoming even more violent.

As it happened, by 2008 economic interests and political interests coincided with this new development in

Zimbabwe's geopolitics: diamonds were the key. Two years earlier a rich alluvial diamond field had been discovered by villagers in the Marange district in the southeast of the country.[12] Initially local people regarded this as a windfall. At first the government allowed the area to be developed privately and by local prospectors. A subsidiary of the De Beers Company had been working in the area, but was replaced by a British-based company, African Consolidated Resources (ACR). Soon, however, ARC was forced to abandon its claim by the Zimbabwean police, who denied the company access to the area. A free-for-all developed, with informal mines springing up across the diamond fields. The government stepped in to grant the state-owned Zimbabwe Mining Development Corporation (ZMDC) exclusive rights to the area, and the local miners were elbowed out. The diamond fields—reputed to be among the richest in the world—were sealed off from November 2006, with not even members of Parliament or diplomats allowed to visit the area.[13]

In February 2007 Mugabe went one step further, declaring that only the government would mine the diamonds.[14] In reality, a range of operators had become involved in a proliferating smuggling operation with the gems being taken out to Lebanon, the United Arab Emirates, India, Pakistan, and Europe. Local agents (mostly Zimbabweans) bought up the gems locally, with the big money made by the main buyers (known as "barons") who lived in Harare, Mozambique, or South Africa and enjoyed political, military, or police protection.[15] Some five hundred syndicates were said to be in operation in November 2008.[16] According to Human Rights Watch, the process was accompanied by extreme violence. This included the establishment of torture camps, gross abuse, and killings. In one government-organized operation in 2008, 1,500 troops encircled freelance miners and massacred over 88. In 2009 the Kimberley Process banned the formal trade of Zimbabwean diamonds, which simply moved to illegal networks. Since there were vast sums of money to be made and Zimbabwe was in the throes of an economic crisis, this was probably unsurprising. Initially the main beneficiaries were police, about six hundred of whom were deployed in the area. One policeman claimed he made as much as $10,000 in bribes and backhanders in just three months.[17]

Mugabe decided that these riches should come under his control, rather than allowing them to be distributed in an arbitrary way among the security services. The president later revealed that he had been briefed on who would be allowed to participate in the exploitation of these reserves. "We had a list of companies applying," Mugabe is quoted as saying. "Finally two of them, Mbada and Canadile, were chosen. They were recommended and I was shown the papers and the proposals."[18] There is no suggestion that the money raised from the mining went to the state. Although there were promises by the Ministry of Mining that the diamond mines would generate $600 million, the Ministry of Finance complained that it had not received the revenue. The finance minister noted, "We are beginning to sound like a broken record in emphasising the need for transparency in the handling of our diamond revenues and, indeed general revenue from the rest of the mining sector."[19] Based on externally available figures, Zimbabwe received more than $1.7 billion from diamond exports from 2010 to 2014, but less than $200 million in taxes, royalties, and dividends were remitted to government.[20]

With the control of the mines allocated by Mugabe to the companies he favored, the Chinese became involved. Before 2003 only three Chinese companies had invested in Zimbabwe. In the next decade the figure rose to sixty-three.[21] An investigation by Global Witness indicated that the Chinese took considerable stakes in the companies involved in the exploitation of the diamonds.[22] There was said to be a complex system of company holdings in a variety of geographical locations, but these companies were, in reality, designed to benefit two groups of people: senior Zimbabweans military officers and Chinese businessmen.[23] The beneficiaries were said to have included (on the Zimbabwean side) Martin Rushwaya, the permanent secretary in the Ministry of Defence; Oliver Chibage, a commissioner of police; and former air vice marshal Robert Mhlanga. The links between the Chinese and Zimbabwe's military were underlined by claims that revenue from one of the companies was used to finance the construction of the country's National Defence College.[24]

It was not long before the relationship with the Chinese deepened. Early in 2010 the *Daily Telegraph*'s veteran Zimbabwe correspondent, Peta Thornycroft, broke the news that a giant runway was being constructed in the diamond fields.[25] The newspaper carried photographs of the airfield, complete with control tower: "Diplomats and analysts believe that the mile-long runway is intended for arms shipments, probably from China, for which troops loyal to President Robert Mugabe would pay on the spot with gemstones from the Chiadzwa diamond mines." Although the airfield allegedly was only designed to allow light aircraft to land, to fly the gems to Harare, it soon became clear that long-range aircraft (an Antonov An-12 cargo plane, with a range of 5,700 km) were landing twice a week.[26] The Antonov brought in members of the Chinese army as well as mining equipment. The plane is also said to have delivered weaponry. Chinese soldiers were reported to have taken control of security of the mining concerns.[27] From Zimbabwe's point of view, it would appear that most of the diamonds were smuggled out of the country, with little benefit accruing to Zimbabwe. As an academic put it: "One can conclude that the security agencies remained the primary, if not the sole, beneficiaries of China's mining of the Marange diamonds."[28]

There is another aspect of Zimbabwe's relationship with the East that must be mentioned, and that is the personal. President Mugabe and his second wife, Grace, found in the East an escape from the worries of everyday life and a playground for their personal pleasures. Zimbabwe's media were full of stories of Grace's extravagance. She has presided over the construction of two ostentatious presidential residences since their marriage in 1996, one of which is known colloquially as "Gracelands." (Such is the extent of her purchase of a particular type of blue ceramic tile, from China, it is now known as "Grace Blue.") She selected a farm northwest of Harare, ordering the elderly couple who owned it off the land.[29] Since then she and her husband have built up a substantial property portfolio abroad.

So extensive did her properties become that since 2002 Commonwealth, European Union, and United States agencies were reportedly investigating Mugabe's wealth around the world.[30] This included a property in the Malaysian capital, Kuala Lumpur, where the family was assured of a safe haven should the situation in Zimbabwe deteriorate.[31] This dates back to the personal and political friendship between the Malaysian prime minister, Dr. Mahathir bin Mohamed, and Mugabe from the 1980s and 1990s. There is another £4 million villa in Hong Kong's New Territories, where their daughter, Bona Mugabe, studied. In recent years ownership of the property has been disputed, with a Taiwanese-born South African citizen claiming that it is only leased to the Mugabes.[32] The Mugabe family also reputedly owns properties in Cape Town, Dubai, and two in Manchester.[33]

During his final years as president, Mugabe spent increasing periods of time outside Zimbabwe, much of which is speculated to have been for medical treatment. Tendai Biti, former finance minister, alleged that in the first six months of 2016 the president clocked up 200,000 kilometers of travel, at a cost of \$80 million.[34] This is said to have included no fewer than ten visits to Singapore. With an entourage of up to forty people, he is said to have taken \$6 million from the Treasury on his trips.[35] This means that he and his family treated the Zimbabwe central bank as their personal ATM. It is impossible to verify the accuracy of these reports. All that can be said is that they have been repeated widely down the years, and there is little to contradict what was said.

7

Mugabe and the People

Robert Mugabe's performance as a political leader was often challenged. There was no shortage of criticism of his authoritarianism, with plenty of evidence of his ruthless determination to acquire, and then hang on to, power. This could be traced back to his earliest days in the liberation movement fighting white Rhodesian rule. No one who witnessed the crushing of his opponents, inside his own party or outside it, could doubt this. Whether it was confronting Joshua Nkomo and the Matabele challenge or the MDC in later years, who could dispute the lengths to which Mugabe would go to eliminate his rivals? Urban Zimbabweans who questioned his authority and farm laborers who supported his political enemies felt the retribution of the security forces. The president's political history is littered with bodies.

At the same time it is important to consider how many political leaders can match his record. Here is a man who took the oath of office on April 17, 1980; he led Zimbabwe for over thirty-seven years. There were plenty of opportunities to oust him through the ballot box. On several occasions (as tables 2 and 3 indicate) the ruling party came close to losing elections, despite evidence of vote rigging. It would also have been possible to resume the armed struggle to confront Mugabe's authoritarian rule. Yet no one succeeded in ousting him before November 2017, nor were there any serious attempts to begin an armed resistance. Only Botswana came close to supporting the MDC as a military force, and even though deeply critical of the Zimbabwean government, Botswana backed away from this option.[1] Mugabe was certainly not a leader who remained at home, for fear of a coup in his absence: quite the opposite. He was reported to have made no fewer than twenty-two foreign visits in the first half of 2015 alone.[2] He sometimes remained no longer than forty-eight hours in Zimbabwe before flying out again. No wonder he was dubbed the "visiting leader"! During the president's time out of the country, all major decisions were put on hold. "When Mugabe goes on holiday, he goes on holiday with the state," said Pedzisai Ruhanya, a political analyst and the director of the research group Zimbabwe Democracy Institute. "Mugabe's behaviour is inconsistent with practices in other countries, with general state practices. This is kind of strange."[3]

This display of self-confidence was not simply the result of an authoritarian state; it is important to consider the sources of his power, which were wider than the elite that clustered around him within the ruling party and the military. Perhaps Mugabe's hold over his

Table 2: Zimbabwe elections for House of Assembly since independence

Date	ZANU-PF vote %	ZANU-PF seats	Next largest party % vote	Next largest party seats	Total seats elected
Feb 1980[a]	63.0	57	ZAPU 24.1	ZAPU 20	100
June/July 1985	77.2	64	ZAPU 19.3	ZAPU 15	100
March 1990	80.5	117	Zimbabwe Unity Movement 17.6	Zimbabwe Unity Movement 2	102
April 1995	81.4	118	Zimbabwe African National Union-Ndonga 6.9	Zimbabwe African National Union-Ndonga 2	120
June 2000	48.6	62	Movement for Democratic Change 47.0	Movement for Democratic Change 57	120
March 2005	59.6	78	Movement for Democratic Change 40.0	Movement for Democratic Change 41	120
2008	46.8	99	Movement for Democratic Change 45.2	Movement for Democratic Change 100	210
July 2013	62.4	159	Movement for Democratic Change 30.3	Movement for Democratic Change 49	210

Source: African Election Database.

Note: Only two largest parties shown, http://africanelections.tripod.com/zw.html#1980_House_of_Assembly_Election.

[a] In the February 1980 election the Rhodesian Front took the 20 seats reserved for whites in Parliament. These reserved seats were abolished in 1987. There are additional seats that are appointed by the president and ex officio members from among the traditional rulers.

Table 3: Presidential elections Zimbabwe

Date	Name	Party	Votes	Percentage of votes
March 23, 1990	Robert Mugabe	ZANU-PF	2,026,976	83.05%
	Edgar Tekere	ZUM	413,840	16.95%
March 17, 1996	Robert Mugabe	ZANU-PF	1,404,501	92.76%
	Abel Muzorewa	UP	72,600	4.80%
	Ndabaningi Sithole	ZANU-Ndonga	36,960	2.44%
March 9–11, 2002	Robert Mugabe	ZANU-PF	1,685,212	56.2%
	Morgan Tsvangirai	MDC	1,258,401	42.0%
	Three other candidates			1% or less
March 29, 2008 (first round)	Morgan Tsvangirai	MDC	1,195,562	47.87%
	Robert Mugabe	ZANU-PF	1,079,730	43.24%
	Simba Makoni		207,470	8.31%
June 27, 2008 (second round)	Robert Mugabe	ZANU-PF	2,150,269	90.22%
	Morgan Tsvangirai	MDC	233,000	9.78%
July 31, 2013	Robert Mugabe	ZANU-PF	2,110,434	61.09%
	Morgan Tsvangirai	MDC-T	1,172,349	33.94%
	Welshman Ncube	MDC-N	92,637	2.68%

own party is partly explained by the veteran opposition politician David Coltart concerning the manner in which the president was treated by cabinet ministers from his own party. Coltart described his own swearing in as a minister in the Government of National Unity and says: "I was struck by how short and frail he seemed. However, from the very first day it was clear that ZANU PF ministers were in awe of him. Aside from reverently referring to him as 'H.E.' (His Excellency), they were painfully obsequious."[4] This went well beyond the traditional respect that is accorded African leaders and elders. It is important to acknowledge that Mugabe retained the affection, respect, and support of a good number of his countrymen and countrywomen. Those who benefited from the land reforms feel they owe him a great deal. He remains, in their eyes, the liberator of their country and the source of the land that they now hold. Mugabe had particularly strong support in Shona areas that benefited from state patronage and remained loyal to ZANU-PF.

Some academics see land reform as a success. "In the biggest land reform in Africa, 6,000 white farmers have been replaced by 245,000 Zimbabwean farmers," argue commentators who support the policy, implicitly denying the nationality of white farmers. The same authors go on to state: "These are primarily ordinary people who have become more productive farmers. The change was inevitably disruptive at first but production is increasing rapidly."[5] The productivity of the new farmers might be questioned; what cannot be disputed is that they owe their new farms and status to the Mugabe government, and the majority of them are duly appreciative.

The same cannot be said of the farmworkers, most of whom lost their homes and livelihoods in the land redistribution. They number, say the authors, 313,000— some permanent and some seasonal.[6] The real question is what happened to them: the unfortunate losers in this traumatic process. Although the evidence is incomplete, Ian Scoones, who has conducted long-term research in an area of southeastern Zimbabwe, suggests some answers. He believes that one in ten received land on the farms that were seized, or further afield. But even those farmworkers who were given farms during the redistribution received much smaller plots of land than other beneficiaries. "Comparing farm worker households to others, we can see that across variables, farm worker households are badly off. They have very small plots of land (average 0.6ha), all of which is cultivated." He concludes: "There is little doubt that former farm workers are extremely poor and often have precarious livelihoods."[7] This is supported by other studies, which indicate that "most of the farm workers face many difficulties with up to two-thirds of them jobless and landless." Some turned to "informal trade, fishing and hunting for survival, gold-panning, and piece-work." Others began selling fruit and vegetables and trading in second-hand clothing on farms and in neighboring towns and mines.[8]

The response of the government was, in the main, that this was someone else's problem—arguing that many of the farmworkers were foreign laborers. The General Agriculture and Plantations Workers Union (GAPWUZ) general secretary, Gift Muti, said he had approached the government on several occasions to ask for assistance for the former farmworkers but to no avail. "They believe that when someone's employment has been terminated, they should go back to where they came from. But the problem is that most of these people are migrant workers, from neighbouring countries such as Malawi, Zambia and Mozambique and the farms are the only homes they know," he said. Muti believed that many farm laborers were left in penury, since they had been deprived of their only source of income and shelter. "Most of these people were ejected from the farms during the summer season, which affected the crops they had planted on their small pieces of land, exposing them to hunger. They are also exposed to the vagaries of the weather, especially the children and women, some of whom are pregnant. They are living in groups by the roadsides and have no access to health care facilities and they are in desperate need of assistance," Muti explained.[9]

The rural population can therefore be divided into those (particularly in the Shona-speaking areas) who were, and are, strong supporters of Robert Mugabe; those who are still skeptical or even hostile (particularly in the Ndebele-speaking areas that were so savagely attacked in the 1980s during the Gukurahundi massacres); and those who remain marginalized, including the former farmworkers (many of whom left for other countries). Despite the losers in these radical reforms, it was a success from President Mugabe's point of view. As Sara Rich Dorman remarked, the land reform program remained the ruling party's "most successful political gambit."[10] It paid dividends for the governing party time and again.

The rural areas have become the bedrock of ZANU-PF's support. Over 70 percent of voters live outside urban areas, and the majority of the country's 210 parliamentary constituencies are rural. It is therefore no surprise that in the 2013 elections an estimated 99.97 percent of potential rural voters were registered, while only about 67.94 percent of the potential urban voters were registered. Zimbabwe's demographic profile is also important. On election day itself the independent Zimbabwe Election Support Network said that urban voters were further "systematically disenfranchised."[11] There is evidence of massive and carefully organized vote rigging in the 2013 elections.[12] In the election there was a substantial discrepancy between the numbers registered in urban versus rural areas, and on polling day itself far more voters were turned away in urban areas than in rural constituencies.[13] There were also considerably higher numbers of assisted rural votes than in the urban areas. This was not simply the product of illiteracy; in many cases, it was also a postelection personal defense strategy in case of a sizable MDC vote. These voters could then prove they were not "sell-outs," and thus avoid vicious retribution by ZANU-PF activists, or loss of access to food handouts and state material support.[14] As a result, the ruling party wins seats in the rural areas, allowing it to control most local councils. The Zimbabwe Election Support Network reported: "ZANU PF is now dominating the country's rural and urban councils after winning 1,493 wards against MDC-Ts 442."

Local Authority: Chiefs and Headmen

The Mugabe government, while retaining the backing of many in the rural areas who benefited from the land redistribution, had another source of support. The traditional tribal systems of governance have been used by the ZANU-PF administration, just as they were under previous Rhodesian governments (when the chiefs were paid employees of the state). Chiefs and headmen have played a major role in the politics of the country since white rule began. This authority is entrenched in law, as John Makumbe has pointed out. "Both the Constitution of Zimbabwe and the Chiefs and Headmen Act provide for various forms of relationships between traditional authorities, particularly chiefs, and local authorities. The rationale behind this arrangement is essentially that traditional leaders play a significant role in the lives of the majority of the African people of Zimbabwe. Traditional leaders are generally accepted as the custodians of customary law and practice, and their support has always been sought by successive regimes since Zimbabwe was colonised."[15]

This relationship has not always been easy: traditional leaders who resisted the colonizers were removed from office. Today they are still seen as the custodians of the land and are represented in Parliament through the Council of Chiefs, which has the right to elect eighteen chiefs who sit in the Senate.[16] Each province has a council of chiefs, which is referred to as the Provincial Assembly. From there they influence government policy both at the local level and through the Ministry of Local Government, at a national level.

Men and women who live in the rural areas are closely controlled by a network of power that begins with central government and descends to village level. This is not just the authority and the power of the state being exercised at the local level: it is also a question of livelihoods. There is a strict control of resources. Anyone who questions ZANU-PF can be deprived of everything from seeds to fertilizers.[17] During droughts or other times of hardship, the Grain Marketing Board can refuse to deal with those considered opponents of the ruling party. Derek Matyszak concluded that this pressure made it all but impossible to stand up to the Mugabe government in the countryside.

> It is clear that the current structures of power in the rural areas have been organized so that the determining authority has been shifted away from democratic institutions, such as Rural District

Councils, to appointed individuals who are beholden to central government in the form of the Ministry of Local Government and the President. . . . With Local Government and the appointment of Provincial Governors currently controlled by ZANU PF politicians, and the high probability that the entire local government structure is largely comprised of individuals that hold explicit partisan loyalty to ZANU PF, it is remarkable that any rural dweller, dependent on these individuals for access to scarce resources, and frequently food, should admit to membership of an opposition political party, even in less politically volatile times than those which currently prevail.[18]

During the 2013 elections Mugabe used these leaders to mobilize the voters. Matyszak says that traditional leaders were "observed marshalling their people to come to polling stations and vote. This could be an indication of intimidation and coercion to make sure people voted in a particular way."[19]

The government's hold over the farming communities was further strengthened through its control over the most important medium of communication: the radio. In cities it is possible to use the internet to bring members of the opposition together. Recently movements such as #ThisFlag and #Tajamuka have used Facebook, Twitter, and WhatsApp to rally Zimbabweans against the Mugabe leadership, but these efforts have been mostly targeted at citizens in urban areas, where internet use is high.[20] In the rural areas, using social media is simply not possible, and radio, which is strictly controlled by the government, is the main source of information. (Furthermore, traditional leaders sit on community radio boards.) As the BBC explains, "Zimbabwe Broadcasting Corporation (ZBC) operates TV and radio stations under the umbrella of state-owned Zimbabwe Broadcasting Holdings (ZBH). Two national private FM radio stations are licensed—one to a company owned by a supporter of Mr Mugabe, the other to a majority state-owned publisher."[21] Independent, overseas-based radio stations do make broadcasts to Zimbabwe, but they are subjected to jamming.

Under the circumstances, it is not difficult to see why the rural areas were such a bastion of support for the Mugabe government. Even those who were not government supporters were bludgeoned into submission: deprived of independent information and subjected to intense pressure from vigilantes and traditional rulers. Aware that their votes were likely to be manipulated, it is perhaps remarkable that so many rural people refused to buckle under and still backed the opposition.

South Africa: Migration and Politics

As Zimbabwe's economic and political crisis deepened, increasing numbers of people fled into South Africa. There they sought sanctuary and work. Sometimes they found one and sometimes both, but all too frequently they were met with hostility. No one knows exactly how many Zimbabweans found homes in South Africa. Figures of 2 or 3 million have been quoted, but these have been criticized as unreliable.[22] The South African census figure for 2011 puts the figure at a little over half a million (515,824).[23] Of course this reflects only the number of Zimbabweans who were "captured" by the official data: the number may be considerably higher, since people living illegally in the country would be unlikely to wish to be enumerated in the official statistics.

Having said this, there is no doubt that they represent a significant population, many of whom have real skills to offer. One study found that 45 percent had a higher education qualification. Among them were engineers, nurses, doctors, journalists, and teachers.[24] Some did very well and made comfortable lives for themselves. Zimbabweans sent home goods that helped their families survive the most difficult of times. They also sent cash: in 2016 around US$704 million was sent in remittances, most of it from South Africa.[25] ZANU-PF's decision to bring in bond notes as an alternative currency, and the restriction on bank withdrawals, make hard currency remittances more problematic.

Not all Zimbabweans landed on their feet: jobs were not easy to find and some immigrants were met with considerable hostility. Many faced attacks and persecution that have become a hallmark of townships across the country. Incoming Zimbabwean migrants posed a direct challenge to South African access to scarce resources: housing, access to education, and jobs in the formal and informal sectors. With high levels of literacy, fluent English, and a migrant's drive to succeed, Zimbabweans increased competition. In 2008 and 2009 there were waves of xenophobic attacks on foreigners, including Somalis, Nigerians, and Mozambicans. In one incident alone, some 3,000 Zimbabweans were forced to flee from the farming region of De Doorns in the Western Cape.[26] Thousands found themselves arrested and deported. Others were driven from their homes in the Alexandria township of Johannesburg, and attacks have continued, intermittently, ever since. At times the South African army has had to intervene to halt the killings.[27]

For Zimbabweans who remembered the help they had given to South Africa's liberation movements, this was a bitter moment indeed. Zimbabweans believe the South African government has been tardy in preventing the attacks, criticizing the authorities for failing to intervene. They put this down to the relationship between the ruling parties. As a Zimbabwean blogger wrote: "The ANC fought hard for democracy in South Africa but it has not used its influence as the ruling party in the regional powerhouse to encourage democratic practices among its neighbours. Instead the party has been cosying up to the Zimbabwean president, Robert Mugabe, despite his record of rigging elections and intimidating opponents."[28]

The role of the South African radical politician Julius Malema is also worth noting. In 2010 he made a trip to Zimbabwe as the head of the ANC's Youth League, at the end of which he released a statement praising Mugabe's land seizures. The Youth League described the program as "courageous and militant" and called on young black South Africans to follow Zimbabwe's example and to engage in agriculture in order to reduce their dependence on white farmers.[29] In 2012 Malema (who had by this time fallen out with President Jacob Zuma) was expelled from the ANC and established his own party, the Economic Freedom Fighters. He said his party looked to Zimbabwe for inspiration. But in recent years he became increasingly critical of ZANU-PF policies. He was quoted as describing Mugabe as an "opportunist" who waited until he was losing power to implement land reform and said that South Africa would never follow these methods.[30] By the end of 2016 Malema was calling for Mugabe to step down. "We love President Mugabe," he declared, "but we need a new leader."[31]

One other group appears to have broken with Mugabe: the war veterans. Once the Zimbabwe National Liberation War Veterans' Association were the most stalwart of the president's supporters.[32] But their loyalty wore thin. The war veterans issued a statement in July 2016 saying they would no longer support Mugabe's political campaigns and accusing the president of abandoning them in favor of ZANU-PF's youth league. "We note, with concern, shock and dismay, the systematic entrenchment of dictatorial tendencies, personified by the president and his cohorts, which have slowly devoured the values of the liberation struggle," the group said in a statement.[33] The government's *Herald* newspaper wrote in an editorial that the nation was "shocked" by the decision, saying that the veterans had joined the "'Mugabe must go' bandwagon."[34] Soon the war veterans were facing the president's wrath. Victor Matemadanda, secretary-general of the Zimbabwe National Liberation War Veterans Association, was arrested and charged with insulting the head of state.[35] In a lengthy interview, a senior member of the war veterans, Douglas Mahiya, explained that they had withdrawn their support because of the corruption within the ruling party. He attacked the ZANU-PF "political commissar" Saviour Kasukuwere, saying that he has a "50-roomed house" yet still "calls himself a Comrade."[36] Behind the differences between the president and the veterans were complex maneuverings within ZANU-PF. As a result, the war veterans found themselves isolated and attacked. Mahiya told the interviewer that his movement was now supporting groups opposing the government, including the #ThisFlag campaign started by Pastor Evan Mawarire.

The Battles for Succession and Control of Levers of Power

Given the progressive meltdown of the Zimbabwean state since 2000, the brief period of stabilization during the Government of National Unity 2009–13, and the renewed slide toward economic malaise since July 2013, Mugabe's survival as leader of ZANU-PF was a source of intense fascination and speculation. From independence onward, he also faced—and faced down—significant challenges from within his party: the factional plots to oust him as leader in the 1980s; the creation of rival political parties—Edgar Tekere's Zimbabwe Unity Movement (ZUM), the desertion of ZANU-PF colleagues to reconstitute ZAPU in 2008, and the creation of Mavamba-Kusile by former finance minister Simba Makoni in 2008; and then the rising challenge posed by the political alliance of Solomon and Joice Mujuru. Despite these threats to his authority, he was repeatedly confirmed as ZANU-PF's presidential candidate at the party's congresses until his resignation in November 2017.

The jockeying for succession went on in earnest for more than fifteen years. ZANU-PF has never formed a homogenous elite, and rival groups fought a bitter campaign in the corridors of power. As veteran journalist and editor Wilf Mbanga remarked in 2013, this protracted battle for succession enabled each faction to build necessary alliances and networks, with promises of a "softer landing" for the inevitable post-Mugabe era. If Mugabe had died suddenly, the resulting power vacuum would have been much more of a problem for these ambitious politicians. The party still contains those who believe in their entitlement to govern—tied directly to the national liberation movement ideal of the dominance of ZANU-PF as the vanguard of historical change. With this conviction comes the need for its continued grip on state power. "The party state is simultaneously a party machine, a vehicle for the upward mobility of party elites and for material accumulation justified ideologically by reference to the historical righteousness of transformation," thus making strategies of indigenization central to this historical tendency.[1] The incoming nationalist elite was primarily motivated by "prospects of upward mobility and accumulation offered by capture of the settler state."[2] Weaving together the emerging class of "patriotic black capitalists" with the party-state ensured this new elite would not develop material independence from ZANU-PF and challenge it. Instead, membership of this party elite ensured "political connectivity."

As has been seen, the 1980s and 1990s didn't quite work out according to the vision outlined by official ZANU-PF socialist ideology. Constrained by the enormous burden of transformation from a war economy, the terms of the Lancaster House settlement, the advice of fellow African leaders, and the demands of the international donor community for economic liberalization, Mugabe's government did not fundamentally alter the capitalist structure of the economy post-1980. Lancaster House meant accepting the principles of the market: a large, white-dominated private sector that provided opportunities for the expanding Zimbabwean black middle class, with the parallel expansion of the public sector offering opportunities for ZANU-PF political patronage to party cadres, provincial leaders, political cronies, and family members.[3] Although Mugabe publicly railed against this rapid entrenchment of corruption within the civil service and party elite, lamenting the loss of a sense and spirit of dedicated service, he did not stop it. In 1983 he publicly criticized the corrupting influence of office:

> Even if the present White owners of property and natural resources were to be replaced by Black owners of property and natural resources, the need for a socialist revolution would still remain urgent. A bourgeoisie does not cease to be exploitative merely because its colour has turned Black or because it is now national rather than foreign. . . . I wish to express my utter dismay at the bourgeois tendencies that are affecting our leadership at various levels of government.[4]

These public criticisms of "daylight robbery" by "socialist deviants" continued. A party Leadership Code was established in 1984, but no one paid much attention to it. Although this lack of "ideological consciousness" apparently offended Mugabe, it was far more important to keep the support of the same elite he was criticizing. Nor did he, or his family, attempt to live by the code. For Mugabe, party unity consistently trumped principle—as seen in his agreement to allow Solomon Mujuru (the main surviving military figure involved in quashing the internal ZANU revolt against Mugabe in Mozambique in 1977–78) to expand his business empire, and in his handling of the Willowgate scandal in the late 1980s (in which cabinet ministers were publicly revealed to be obtaining new cars at reduced cost, before selling them on at greatly inflated prices). The suicide of Maurice Nyagumbo (Mugabe's old cell mate and long-standing friend) after Willowgate deeply affected Mugabe; there-after, there would be limits to calling supportive colleagues to account.[5]

On Mugabe's watch, the pattern of personal enrichment of key members of ZANU-PF—ministers, MPs, Central Committee members, and high-ranking civil servants—crucially extended to the security services. They took full advantage of economic liberalization in the 1990s, as the political elite accelerated their strategies of "shameless predation" and accumulation, in the name of "indigenization."[6] As we have indicated, the war in the Democratic Republic of Congo injected new life into the activities of Zimbabwean party-state military entrepreneurs involved in transportation, mining, armaments production, and timber extraction.[7] From 2000, the revolutionary land program also saw a massive transfer to politically connected elites:

> [A] 2,200 strong politically connected elite controls close to half the land seized from white farmers, with President Mugabe, his wife, ZANU-PF Cabinet ministers, senior military officers, provincial governors, senior party officials, chiefs, and judges owning nearly 5 million hectares of agricultural land, including wildlife conservancies and plantations. . . . Mugabe and his wife . . . owned 14 farms (extending to 16,000 hectares. . . . Overall, 90% of the nearly 200 army officers from the rank of Major to Lieutenant-General owned farms, replicated through the air force, police, prison service, and CIO [Central Intelligence Organisation].[8]

The discovery of alluvial diamonds in the Marange field, together with the creation of the Government of National Unity, intensified the determination of the ZANU-PF political-military elite to tighten their control over the diamond fields. This was not simply for purposes of personal accumulation, but also to ensure party funds for future elections, thereby negating the European Union's targeted international economic and financial sanctions.

This is the picture of "an arrogant and parasitical political/military elite determined to cling onto state power, and access to wealth that this confers"[9]—with Mugabe as president at its center. Mugabe's frenetic pattern of international travel on supposed state business earned him the sobriquet "President of the Skies." However, party officials in the office of the president and the cabinet exploited this grandstanding to their own advantage. The president's office is not audited, unlike other Zimbabwean government departments; officials deliberately filled Mugabe's international diary to enable them to draw generous per diem allowances.[10] There is also a particular long-established crossover between business interests and income raised from individual party membership. Since 2000, failure to hold a ZANU-PF membership card has become increasingly dangerous at election times, as well as negatively affecting employment and prospects for bidding on government projects. At the same time, Mugabe became adept at wooing corporate largesse for the party. In 2010, he was actively courting the largest banks in Zimbabwe, as well as leaders of industry, "exchang[ing] laughter and light hearted banter" over tea and sandwiches,[11] as a direct bid for business to fund the party's approaching Congress.

Just as there are many paradoxes in the state of Zimbabwe, this was the paradox of Mugabe: the aesthete and austere "headmaster," condoning rampant accumulation. How did he square this circle? Was he simply a 24-carat hypocrite? Like all things in Zimbabwe, the answer is complicated, shaped by his determination to achieve the "decolonization" of his country by expunging white influence and control and by a determined refusal to listen to liberal whites. His original socialist-oriented rhetoric of "the masses" was replaced by "indigenous Zimbabweans"—a permutation (or corruption, take your pick) of ZANU-PF's declared agenda at independence. This was "left populist" cosmology. It is interesting that since the mid-2000s Mugabe increasingly delivered his public speeches in Shona rather than in English, something he never used to do. By this point, the Zimbabwean revolution was depicted as the "Third Chimurenga"—the final stage of the liberation struggle against white oppression, to address supposed unfinished business of decolonization and indigenous control. Only then would Zimbabwe achieve "true, total independence." At this stage, pigmentation and nation were always going to trump class material redistribution, with socialism pushed into the distant future.[12]

In this mind-set and worldview, strategies of accumulation by Zimbabwean elites—with Mugabe's rapacious wife at the forefront—were preferable to white dominance. The revolutionary transformation of the country—well, that was always going to take time, and inevitably there would be social groups that would be losers. It is hard to judge whether Mugabe genuinely believed that the targeted international sanctions against a specific list of ZANU-PF elite were responsible for the economic hardships of Zimbabwean citizens. It may well be he came to believe his own self-justificatory rhetoric; he would not be the first leader to do this. He also took pains to keep his avaricious wife happy, the woman who had given him three children. But the contradictions of all this were evident, even blatant—his occasional rages on the lack of probity were Olympic-standard moral gymnastics, given his reluctance to have a full land audit (because he would likely face personal embarrassment) and in considering the press reports on elite corruption scandals. Mugabe also profoundly believed in the overriding need for party unity and for ZANU-PF dominance of structures and institutions. The process of ZANU-PF gaining control over the state, and party-business crossovers, paralleled Mugabe's government's vicious repression of the political opposition. Personal factors and power politics defeated personal integrity.

All of this suggested Mugabe was the ultimate arbiter of power. Over the years, he had certainly needed to maneuver skillfully to maintain this position. Repeated challenges brought out the ruthless side of his political and personal nature, as his former colleagues increasingly took their criticisms into the public space: Ibbo Mandaza, Enos Nkala, Edgar Tekere, Eddison Zvobgo (the Harvard-educated neoliberal lawyer, purged in the ZANU-PF party Congress in December 2000), Wilfred Mhanda (a former leader in the revolutionary struggle, and subsequently a progressive critic with the Liberators' Platform Group), Didymus Mutasa (formerly ZAPU), John Nkomo (former ZANU-PF chairperson),

Simba Makoni. At the same time, the Zezuru interest group—with its well-organized and aggressive steering committee known as the Group of 24—was intent on ensuring that it won privileges and dominance for its ethnic members. This group had seen Sally Mugabe as an impediment to its ambitions in the 1980s and was determined, after her death in 1992, that she would be replaced by a more pliant woman.[13] Mugabe also antagonized many Shona politicians in ZANU-PF by advancing members of his own clan; thus an ethnically based undercurrent of anti-Mugabe sentiment complicated the political picture.[14] The squabbling among rival ZANU-PF factions became increasingly bitter because the financial prizes were (and remain) potentially so great and the *Mafikizolo* (a small number of the wealthy ruling elite) were pitted against the old-style politicians from the liberation struggle era.

In 2008 ZANU-PF experienced its first defeat in the parliamentary elections, yet within five years it had come "roaring" back. Mugabe's part in this remarkable turnaround of his party's fortunes is "both straightforward and complicated."[15] He had insisted on holding these "harmonized" elections despite the failure to agree to a new constitution. After the defeat, he did not appear in public for a month. For two days, many observers thought he was on the brink of resigning the presidency. But while Mugabe had the option of considering retiring quietly in "one of several Asian countries" and money wouldn't be a problem, the same was not true for his senior ZANU-PF colleagues who could not hide behind the claims of immunity of a former head of state. "Mugabe's security chiefs were more vulnerable to prosecution than the President himself, as they had carried out the atrocities and could not deploy the defence Mugabe often uses during intimate conversations—that he did not know what was being done in his name."[16]

Was Mugabe's silence then a calculated tactic to draw out internal ZANU-PF potential challengers, and to see how far these rivals might go? He was past master at creating situations that drew critics into the open, only to flatten them. Mugabe's seeming vacillation, then, hammered home that they were all in the same boat, confirming his supposed indispensability. While the announcement of the election result was delayed, Mugabe and the Joint Operations Command (controlling the security services)[17] used the hiatus to launch a two-pronged strategy: (1) using the state-run press to float the idea of a power-sharing agreement (on the Kenyan model), and (2) manipulating the voting figures while launching a wave of brutal intimidation to ensure Mugabe's victory in the second round.

The Global Political Agreement (GPA), which shared power between the parties from 2008 to 2013, then allowed ZANU-PF the space to regroup. In the narrowed political arena of decision makers, Mugabe politically outmaneuvered the Government of National Unity's prime minister, Morgan Tsvangirai. The president appointed more ministers than originally agreed

(41, rather than the originally agreed 31), along with leading civil servants, diplomats, the attorney general, the governor of the Reserve Bank, and the police commissioner.[18] While his party re-energized its grassroots organization and support, ZANU-PF kept control of the security services, as MDC squandered its access to power and remained fatally divided between two rival factions. But this pact with the opposition came at considerable costs to ZANU-PF party unity.

Since 2000 there had also been a "creeping coup" in the militarization of the country's administration, as the securo-crats were absorbed into the upper echelons of decision making. In Paul Moorcraft's view, this fusion of political and military power within ZANU-PF had long been the key to Mugabe's political longevity. However, it was not simply that Mugabe called the shots, or that ZANU-PF dominated the security sector.[19] Zimbabwe under Mugabe was the epitome of a neopatrimonial state. This is not a system dominated and dictated by the personal whim of one man, exercising power through an informal system of rule. It incorporates a particular set of power relations with the trappings of a more liberal institutional system—Parliament, the judiciary, and a constitution. Therefore, power is not simply concentrated in the president's office. By now Mugabe was woven in a matrix of corrupt economic, political, and military networks, a veritable web of codependency. He maintained the uneasy balance between the squabbling and increasingly hostile factions within his party. Norma Kriger has argued that "the different factions within ZANU-PF [were] held together chiefly by a shared vested interest in preventing the 'opposition' parties in the [GPA], and in particular, MDC-T (Tsvangirai) from coming to power as a result of democratizing reforms."[20] Furthermore, during the Global Political Agreement, ZANU-PF moved from formal domination of state institutions to informal and parallel structures as Mugabe and the party concentrated on the business of being reelected, using state control of the media to portray MDC as out of touch. No wonder Tsvangirai was outmaneuvered.

After their surprising defeat in the July 2013 elections, the deeply divided factions of the MDC appeared essentially irrelevant. The battle within ZANU-PF over who was to succeed Mugabe began in earnest. This was a no-holds-barred contest. Indeed, this factional infighting was strongly reminiscent of the ZANU movement in the liberation period. Vicious personal politics also entered the picture in the form of Mugabe's second wife, Grace. Whereas in the 1990s Grace Mugabe had not taken a prominent political role, from this point on, this dramatically altered. For the past decade she had been gatekeeper of Mugabe's diary, and thus the effective controller of access and flows of information reaching the elderly president.

By early 2016, party internecine struggles reached such a pitch that observers were warning the country risked descending into civil war.[21] The principal contenders both had impeccable revolutionary hero credentials: Joice Mujuru, wife of the former ZANLA commander and leading Zimbabwean business entrepreneur General Solomon Mujuru;[22] and Emmerson Mnangagwa, former minister of defense and a man with excellent connections to the security forces and intelligence services, and the Karanga, who want "their turn to eat," to use the Kenyan expression. At independence, Joice Mujuru was the youngest cabinet member, and held continued office until her appointment as vice president in 2004, a move that appeared to anoint her as front-runner to succeed Mugabe. However, Mujuru's power base was dramatically undercut by her husband's mysterious death in 2011. She then fell foul of Grace Mugabe, who had contrived her own appointment in 2014 as head of the influential ZANU-PF Women's League (a position previously held by Sally Mugabe, and one which also put her in the Politburo). Grace Mugabe used this platform to launch a series of vituperative attacks on the vice president. These increasingly lurid accusations included witchcraft (a powerful accusation in traditional Shona culture) and attempting to poison her husband. In the Harare rumor mill, there were tales of "bugged conversations and secret videos showing the vice president in unseemly attire, [and] whisperings of hit men hired in Israel and South Africa."[23] Grace Mugabe didn't pull her punches—unlike her husband, who had long been known for his subtle, ambiguous barbs as he verbally pulverized opponents.[24] (The irony of President Mugabe conferring PhD degrees on both women at the same ceremony at the University of Zimbabwe in September 2014 was not lost on the audience. However, unlike Grace Mugabe, there was no doubt that Mujuru had earned hers.)[25] While Mugabe stayed quiet, the state-run media amplified the First Lady's accusations.

A distinct pattern emerged of vicious infighting and verbal public brawling, culminating in Mugabe's pronouncements calling for an end to the war, and endorsement at the annual ZANU-PF Congress of the senior party lineup. In the meantime, Mugabe regularly reshuffled the cabinet. In 2015 it was enlarged to over seventy-two ministers, "each of whom receives large salaries and allowances, vehicles, housing, and special staff."[26] The ZANU-PF internecine struggle culminated in Joice Mujuru's summary dismissal from the cabinet and expulsion from ZANU-PF in April 2015. This was accompanied by a purge of seven other Mujuru supporters from the cabinet, along with powerful provincial officials. Defiantly, Mujuru founded a new political party, Zimbabwe People First (ZPF), and took her arguments to the diaspora and international audiences.

There was much speculation around Grace Mugabe's own presidential pretensions, and she was certainly determined to protect her substantial property and financial portfolio in Zimbabwe, Dubai, and the Far East, as well as her children's inheritance. This meant she retained a powerful emotional lever over

Mugabe in his responsibilities as a father, as well as her own survival instincts. In 2015 these hints of her possible ambitions excited a storm of media interest. Grace Mugabe was supported by a younger generation in the Politburo and provincial officials, known as Generation 40 or G40.[27] A "Million Man March" in May 2016—with its waving banners of "Vote Comrade Mugabe: This is the final battle for total control," and its posters reading "We Love Our Mother" above images of Grace Mugabe—mobilized ZANU-PF youth brigades around G40, rather than the war veterans. As the highly experienced Zimbabwean analyst Brian Raftopoulos points out, "The absence of employment alternatives for youths makes them extremely vulnerable to such mobilisation by various party structures."[28] It was a blatant political statement of the street, to prepare the ground for the 2018 elections. On July 26, 2017, the First Lady went further: at a meeting of ZANU-PF's women's wing, she publicly challenged her husband to name his preferred successor to end the deepening divisions over the future ZANU-PF leadership, arguing this was the trend in other African countries.[29] Mugabe did not respond.

Emmerson Mnangagwa's own fortunes fluctuated markedly from 2000. A fellow veteran of the liberation movement, he too left ZAPU for the newly formed ZANU in 1963, and had led the first group of ZANLA cadres to China to be trained in sabotage techniques. After finishing his military training, Mnangagwa returned to Tanzania in May 1964, where he and other returning ZANU guerrillas formed the Crocodile Gang. Mnangagwa was captured after blowing up a railway train in Rhodesia, and only narrowly escaped the death sentence. The Rhodesian authorities mistakenly thought he was under sixteen, although Mnangagwa was about twenty-one at the time. He spent ten years in jail and was released in 1974 as part of the "unity talks" amnesty. In Mozambique, he was elected special assistant to the president at the 1977 Chimoio congress—which meant he was the military and civilian representative of the party. He also accompanied Mugabe to the Lancaster House negotiations. Mnangagwa served in every cabinet until he lost his constituency seat to MDC in the 2000 election. He was brought back by Mugabe to be Speaker of Parliament. In 2014–15, he seemed to be complicit in the First Lady's coarse but effective crusade against Joice Mujuru, and in 2014 Mugabe appointed him vice president, following Mujuru's dismissal. However, the alliance of convenience between "the Crocodile" and the First Lady then descended into another toxic and highly public struggle, with press reports of mysterious burglaries of Mnangagwa's office and intimidation of his supporters within ZANU-PF. His supporters within the party and its provincial structures were nicknamed "Team Lacoste" (from the French designer label's crocodile motif). In 2016 there were street brawls between rival youth brigades supporting the Mnangagwa and Grace Mugabe factions. Furthermore, Central Intelligence Organisation agents were reported to be watching the movements of current and former ZANU-PF elites on Mnangagwa's behalf. Intelligence officers also continued to threaten opposition leaders.[30] As a member of the Karanga community, Mnangagwa is firmly opposed to Zezuru dominance within ZANU-PF. He and other Karanga ZANU-PF politicians remained determined to prevent a Zezuru succession, which would limit their access to state assets—a key factional issue within the party.

From late 2016 Mnangagwa increasingly took over the day-to-day management of Politburo meetings and cabinet discussions, to the evident boiling frustration of his rivals, who publicly accused him of disrespect of "The Boss" and, in front of Mugabe, called for Mnangagwa to be fired.[31] For all his charm and reputation for being good company, Mnangagwa remained an extremely tough and ruthless politician—in the 1980s he once repeatedly punched a fellow ZANU-PF cabinet minister, to "discipline" him.[32] He had also been the key strategist behind ZANU-PF's successful election campaign in 2013. Furthermore, Mnangagwa was always careful to underline publicly his political loyalty and personal indebtedness to Mugabe. He played on the myth that he was the leader of the Crocodile Commando, claiming (wrongly) to be the first ZANU guerrilla group to kill a white farmer.

Mugabe had long been the master of playing rival factions off against each other, using a combination of intimidation, abuse of state resources, and violence to achieve his aims. "His specialism [was] to set up ambitious underlings in the ruling ZANU-PF party to fight so that he [could] eventually chide them for factionalism and push aside the likely winner, perpetually eliminating potential rivals." However, by late 2017 this image of the ringmaster was diminishing with his advancing age and declining health, along with his ability to "defuse the bombs he plants."[33] Time was not on Mugabe's side. While his sycophantic supporters argued that he remained alert and lucid, he had repeatedly been filmed dozing off in long public meetings. Yet in the view of Ibbo Mandaza, "He [did] not have the word 're-tire' in his vocabulary."[34]

Mugabe himself continued to blow hot and cold on his possible successor—for example, in January 2016 he dismissed Mnangagwa's opponents as wasting their time in their efforts to stop him from becoming Zimbabwe's next leader,[35] yet in his customary birthday interview with Zimbabwe Broadcasting Corporation in February 2017, Mugabe scoffed that there was not one person among his ambitious lieutenants who was worthy of succeeding him. This was promptly pounced on by Team Lacoste, which declared that they would now publicly campaign for Mnangagwa to be Mugabe's designated successor.

Eaten by the Crocodile?

The image of an "aging Godfather of a feuding Mafia family"[1] was a compelling one, but by late 2017 it was unraveling. The president's relationship with his core supporters among the war veterans had been deteriorating for some time. Three years earlier a leading member of the war veterans organization, Jabulani Sibanda, was taken to court for daring to suggest that Grace Mugabe was plotting to take over the leadership of the country through a "bedroom coup."[2] Sibanda was accused of declaring that "power was not sexually transmitted." Sibanda lost his position, but gradually the veterans became increasingly vocal in their criticism of Grace Mugabe and—by inference—of the president himself.

In August 2017 Mnangagwa fell ill and had to be airlifted to South Africa for treatment. Suggestions that he had been poisoned by ice cream from Grace Mugabe's dairy were met by the First Lady's angry rebuttals, broadcast on state television.[3] Relations swiftly deteriorated. On November 4, Grace Mugabe was loudly booed by a crowd when she took the microphone at a rally in Bulawayo. She attacked Mnangagwa, accusing him of being the "root cause of factionalism." When he spoke, the president departed from his prepared text to address the booing, and threatened to fire Mnangagwa, whom he blamed for the crowd's display of disrespect.[4] A point of no return had been reached. On November 6, following lengthy ZANU-PF party meetings, Mugabe denounced Mnangagwa for showing "traits of disloyalty." He was summarily removed from his position as vice president and expelled from the party, along with fifteen members of ZANU-PF's provincial committees aligned with Team Lacoste. This apparently cleared the way for Grace Mugabe to be appointed as a vice president at the forthcoming ZANU-PF party congress in mid-December. (She was also in charge of the committee overseeing the ZANU-PF 2018 election campaign preparations.)

The sacking marked a seismic shift in Zimbabwean politics. Mnangagwa had been Mugabe's closest ally, one of only two cabinet ministers who had served since the original cabinet in 1980. This proved to be a fatal error by Mugabe. For someone who had carefully weighed his options and only struck when he was certain of success, it was an uncharacteristic overreach. Perhaps Grace Mugabe's impatience and crude political maneuvering skewed his judgment, clouded by hubris and extreme old age. Perhaps he had come to believe himself to be indispensable to the success of the ZANU-PF project, a belief strengthened by his disdain for those junior to him. Whatever the reason, the sacking of Mnangagwa was the straw that broke the camel's back: party loyalists, war veterans, and the military turned on Mugabe, united in resisting Grace Mugabe's vaunting ambition and her allies in the G40 movement and among youth leaders, who were deemed greedy and disrespectful.

For Mnangagwa, it was a moment of intense personal danger, and he knew it. He had no desire to join the long list of former Mugabe loyalists who had died in mysterious circumstances. Moments after he was ousted, the security officers assigned to protect Mnangagwa and his family were withdrawn. He was told his life was in danger. "Security personnel, who are friendly to me, warned me that plans were underfoot to eliminate me once arrested and taken to a police station," Mnangagwa later declared. "It was in my security interest to leave the country immediately."[5] The former vice president sought sanctuary abroad. His initial attempt to fly to South Africa was thwarted, as a mining company refused to allow its private jet to be used in the escape. Plan B was put into operation, and a convoy of cars headed from Harare toward the Mozambique border. Mnangagwa's car was halted at the border, where his remaining security guards prevented police from searching the vehicles. After a brief scuffle, the vehicle was allowed to proceed and he crossed into Mozambique and safety.[6]

The Reuters news agency pieced together how events then unfolded from COI memoranda and reports from Harare, Moscow, and Beijing.[7] From Mozambique Mnangagwa left for South Africa, with some suggestions that he might have visited China en route. Zimbabwe's military chief, General Constantino Chiwenga, had already left for Beijing, having previously fallen out with Mugabe. According to Reuters, in late October, Mugabe summoned Chiwenga to a showdown. "Mugabe confronted the army chief about his ties to Mnangagwa and told him that going against Grace would cost him his life. . . . Chiwenga was warned by Mugabe that it is high time for him to start following. He mentioned to Chiwenga that those fighting his wife are bound to die a painful death," the intelligence report said. At the same meeting, Mugabe also ordered Chiwenga to pledge allegiance to Grace. He declined. "Chiwengwa refused to be intimidated. He stood his ground over his loyalty to Mnangagwa," the report said.

Mugabe was already concerned that he was facing a coup before this confrontation with Chiwenga. A CIO intelligence report dated October 23 noted, "Mugabe was openly told by senior CIOs that the military is not going to easily accept the appointment of Grace. He was warned to be ready for civil war." On November 5 Chiwenga left for a prearranged official visit to China. The

Chinese, who had backed Mugabe and ZANU-PF from the start of the liberation struggle and had very considerable investments in the country, were important to get onside as the dramatic events unfolded. The following day Mnangagwa was sacked.

From this point, the power struggle inside ZANU-PF developed into a complex and multilayered chess board, with the involvement of key international and regional actors, each with a stake in the outcome. Chiwenga's visit to China culminated in a meeting with the Chinese defense minister, Chang Wanquan, in Beijing on November 10. According to the Reuters report, citing two sources with knowledge of their discussions, Chiwenga asked if China would agree not to interfere if he took temporary control in Zimbabwe to remove Mugabe from power. (The PRC government is particularly important as a lender of last resort, given the parlous state of Zimbabwe's balance of payments.) "Chang assured him Beijing would not get involved and the two also discussed tactics that might be employed during the de facto coup." It appears that South Africa's President Zuma gave similar assurances, in that he gave sanctuary to Mnangagwa. According to *Africa Confidential,* once in South Africa, Mnangagwa, Chiwenga, and Chris Mutsvangwa, the war veterans leader and former ambassador to China, "talked to local security officials about the implications of their military action in Harare. . . . They were given assurances of non-intervention by South Africa so long as the action didn't spill over the borders and remained 'broadly constitutional.'"[8]

As the spectre of another bout of hyperinflation loomed, the Zimbabwean military, together with Mnangagwa, were acutely aware of Mugabe's declining ability to pay the salaries of soldiers and police and thereby ensure their loyalty.[9] Immediately after Mnanagawa's sacking, the military activated a "Code Red" alert, its highest level of preparedness. A coup to remove President Mugabe began to be rolled out. It was vital for Zimbabwe's military, security services, and party veterans that this should be seen as legitimate by their neighbors in the Southern African Development Community (chaired by South Africa) and the African Union, whose 2007 charter proscribes "illegal means of accessing or maintaining power."[10] This nexus of elites who had surrounded Mugabe since the liberation struggle era were also determined to ensure that the regime that replaced him would not threaten their own accumulated wealth and vested interests. Both these objectives were reflected in the coup's code name: "Operation Restore Legacy."

Initially, the president's overthrow seemed to proceed remarkably smoothly. ZBC, the state-controlled television station, was surrounded, as was the presidential residence. Armored vehicles and sufficient troops were deployed to prevent the police or the Presidential Guard from interrupting events. Key ministers were detailed, with a claimed minimum of fuss or violence.

(According to his lawyers, the minister of finance, Ignatius Chombo, was stripped naked and beaten while in detention; and the leading G40 ministers Jonathan Moyo and Saviour Kasukuwere sought emergency refuge in the presidential compound.) Grace Mugabe herself was taken into military custody. Only one obstacle stood in the way of an orderly transfer of power: the president himself. Despite being faced with overwhelming force—a tank remained parked outside his residence—and being placed under house arrest, Mugabe refused to resign.

The massive street demonstrations in Harare and Bulawayo on Saturday, orchestrated and sanctioned by the military, posed a moment of danger to the architects of the "soft coup": the multiple agendas of different groups in the elated crowds, united only in their desire to see Mugabe step down, risked unleashing a "democratizing coup," which had never been ZANU-PF's purpose. On Sunday, November 19, ZANU-PF's Central Committee removed Mugabe as party leader and ZANU-PF's designated presidential candidate for the 2018 elections. Grace Mugabe and the G40 "cabal" were summarily thrown out of the party, and their supporters in provincial committees were also ejected. Mnangagwa was reinstated as vice president designate and ZANU-PF's proposed presidential candidate.

When Mugabe was finally persuaded to address the nation that evening, he was surrounded by the military hierarchy, all of whom proceeded to salute him and treat him with respect bordering on reverence. In a surreal piece of political theater, his long-term adviser and confessor, the Roman Catholic priest Fidelis Mukonori, sat next to him, as if poised to deliver the last rites for Mugabe's long and controversial political career.[11] Mugabe's speech acknowledged mistakes, but said nothing about resignation. His delivery was hesitant and faltering, but while the text contained hints of contrition, the overall message was defiant. Crucially, it exonerated the military for their action, bringing this back within the elastic bounds of constitutional behavior. To a stunned nation and expectant international press corps, Mugabe declared: "I, as the president of Zimbabwe and their commander in chief, do acknowledge the issues they have drawn my attention to, and do believe that these were raised in the spirit of honesty and out of deep and patriotic concern for the stability for our nation and for the welfare of our people."[12]

The rambling twenty-minute address left the ZANU-PF hierachy furious, but impotent. Nothing, it appeared, would force Mugabe to relinquish power while at the same time retaining the necessary myth of a legitimate transfer of control. It begged the questions: Was he convinced that he could once again outmaneuver his enemies? Or was this deeply delusional behavior the unraveling of a once formidable strategist and tactician in extreme old age? Or, thirdly, had Mugabe done a deal with the army to stay on in power?

The onus was now on ZANU-PF to move quickly. Impeachment proceedings in Parliament were initiated on Tuesday, with the planned arrival of key southern African leaders (South Africa's President Jacob Zuma and Angola's President João Lourenço) and long-retired Zambian leader Kenneth Kaunda. Mnangagwa issued an open call for Mugabe to resign "or be humiliated." Only then did Mugabe finally relent. This time nothing was left to chance, and his short letter of resignation was read out by the Speaker of the Parliament, who had just convened impeachment proceedings. The coup leaders were determined that Mugabe would not be allowed access to radio or television again, and with good reason. As a perceptive observer noted:

> Among Mugabe's most effective instruments, and one that he deployed frequently, was his extraordinary voice. It may seem odd to outsiders, but Mugabe's speeches were one of the ways he held sway over his country. They contained sweeping phrases invoking Zimbabwe's fifteen-year liberation struggle against the Rhodesian settler regime of Ian Smith. He employed rhetorical devices that made his words weapons: the amplification and over-enunciation; the deliberate, timed pauses between words; the elongation of the second syllables of certain words, such as "among," "indeed," "comported"; and the evocation of emotion

through lilting inflection at unexpected moments. His is the most recognizable voice in Zimbabwe not only because he was the only leader that generations have known but also because he speaks like no one else.[13]

The relief felt by his successor, Mnangagwa, and his associates in the military and the security services was palpable. There had been private fears that the opposition might try to manipulate the joint committee process to their own advantage, demanding free and fair elections and security sector reform as the price for their cooperation. In his inaugural address, President Mnangagwa went out of his way to pay tribute to his predecessor, addressing him as "a father, mentor, comrade-in-arms and my leader."[14] He went on to strike all the appropriate notes: calling for reconciliation, preserving the land redistribution while saying that white farmers would be compensated for the farms they had lost, and declaring that elections would proceed in 2018. Mnangagwa also called for corruption to "stop forthwith," following up three days later with a three-month amnesty for the repatriation of stolen wealth. The irony of this action was not lost on Zimbabweans and external observers, since the new president had been named in a UN report, published in 2002, as part of an "elite network" that had "transferred ownership of at least US\$5 billion of assets from the State mining sector to private companies under its control."[15] Mnangagwa was said to have personally been involved in a circle of diamond dealers who "turned Harare into a significant illicit diamond-trading centre."

Notwithstanding Mnangagwa's deeply compromised past and the continuation of ZANU-PF's grip on power, Mugabe's departure was truly the end of an era. After 13,731 days of Mugabe's long and controversial leadership, power had finally been passed on. Officially, Mugabe was to be treated as a respected figure, with the loss of office softened by promises of $10 million to ease his departure from office.[16] Unofficially, he (and his wife) were granted immunity from prosecution and permitted to stay in the country with the opportunity to travel overseas for any necessary medical treatment. His birthday has been declared a national holiday, Harare International Airport has been renamed in his honor, and it was announced he would offer advice to the new leadership as an elder.

Yet, many in Zimbabwe will remember Mugabe far less fondly. The thousands of amaNdebele who lost family members (innocent civilians, ZAPU activists, and former ZIPRA fighters) during the brutal atrocities of the extended Gukurahundi campaign in the 1980s have no reason to thank Mugabe. The opposition parties whose activities were suppressed and whose attempts to participate in the electoral process were thwarted have bitter memories of their former head of state. The millions driven into humiliating exile in South Africa and beyond—a number that vastly exceeds those driven into exile by the Rhodesian regime—will recall Mugabe with little affection.

It is perhaps worth recalling that at independence in 1980 Mugabe inherited one of the most economically diverse countries in Africa. Yet he presided over a period of hyperinflation that at one point in 2008 "hit the rate of 231,000,000%. The currency had to be denominated in notes as large as the $100trn Zimbabwe-dollar bill—worth about 40 cents at the time of its demise."[17] The MDC economist Eddie Cross calculated that at independence real GDP per capita in Zimbabwe was about US$3,600; by 2017 it stood at about US$1,000. As a comparison, in 1980 GDP per capita in Botswana was about US$1,500; in 2017 this statistic was US$13,000 per capita.[18] By the end of 2017, formal unemployment in Zimbabwe was estimated at over 90 percent. By stubbornly clinging to office, Mugabe significantly compromised his legacy in the region. Once seen as a leading member of the fight to end white rule in neighboring South Africa, in the eyes of some commentators he undermined the potency of the liberation myth itself. Liberation mythology "has hobbled democracy, justice and development in our region," remarked South African journalist Mondli Makhanya. "Once in power, liberation movements inculcate in the people the belief that they are holy and are the only institutions capable of looking after the countries they run. Armed with this religious message, they proceed to do all manner of things unholy and work against the people and their freedom."[19]

Mugabe proved a deeply complex and contradictory individual. A man capable of great charm and considerate hospitality, he was most likely responsible for the assassination of opponents and critics (such as the suspicious death of the ZANLA military leader, Josiah Tongogara, in a car crash in December 1979 and the mysterious killing of General Solomon Mujuru) and ultimately for mass murder of his own people, the economic decline of his country, sizable outward migration, and enormous suffering brought on by starvation and the collapse of the health care system. He was a dedicated revolutionary who deeply admired Queen Elizabeth II and appreciated Savile Row suits. A man of personal conviction, he oversaw the rampant theft of his country's assets and enabled the rapacious spending habits of his second wife and extended family. As a political manipulator, he consolidated his personal power through structures and personalities, through rivals and antagonists who "worked towards the leader." And as a political manager, he oversaw ZANU-PF's policies as a rural-based movement that produced Zimbabwe's deprivation but presented itself as the solution, through largesse, food handouts, and access to land for voters.

What now for Zimbabwe? Robert Mugabe caused profound damage to his country, which will take generations to address. By overseeing a program of revolution and decolonization, he indeed saw the socioeconomic transformation of his country, but not enough Zimbabweans benefited. Land reform was much needed—make no mistake about that—but the mode and means of this transformation tore apart rural welfare and employment structures, and impoverished millions. The return to growth in the agriculture sector has been partial, and thus food security remains compromised, complicated by a severe drought in 2015–16. Meanwhile, the extraordinary windfall of the discovery of alluvial diamonds, conservatively estimated at $16 billion, was comprehensively looted and lost to the exchequer. The once-admired Zimbabwe health care system has been gutted, with HIV/Aids prevalence at an estimated 13.5 percent (1 in 5 adults is thought to be HIV positive, with girls and young women aged fifteen to twenty-four deemed to be the most vulnerable group), and infant mortality rates at 25.78 per 1,000 births.[20] The once widely admired tertiary education and training sector is severely battered. Currently there are an estimated 3.5 million Zimbabweans living outside the country.

Mugabe oversaw a fundamental shift in the human geography of his country. The majority of the population remains rural; there has been an important reconfiguration of social structures, a quiescent trade union sector, and the church hierarchy remained shamefully quiet until the Zimbabwe Council of Churches' open letter in early November 2017, calling for his resignation. Commentators have noted the rapid acceleration of civil society activism via social media. There is an undercurrent of debate on the need for an amnesty: Should a truth and reconciliation commission be established to address the violence and oppression of the past? And, unlike South Africa, can this be achieved without legal retribution? Can reconciliation be achieved without justice? There are no easy answers. Indeed, could such questions even be raised once ZANU-PF firmly reasserted its control and a narrative of "political stability," with the opposition, yet again, shut out of any possibility of a broader government of national unity and effectively sidelined? In essence, Zimbabwe now faces ZANU-PF's version of "government," in sharp contrast to the opposition parties' desire for "governance" through genuinely free and fair elections, and a free media space.

Zimbabwe became a rogue state under Mugabe's watch, seen in the use of military and extrajudicial force during his time in office, and his collaboration with Libya's former leader, Colonel Qaddafi (which included allowing terrorist training camps on Zimbabwean soil). His political machinations—a US diplomatic cable, published by Wikileaks in 2007, described him as a "brilliant tactician"—were directly associated with his acute reading of people, an ability to spot flaws in his adversaries' argument, and a profound conviction of his own intellectual superiority and authority. A remote and distant figure who would lecture his junior colleagues while standing behind his desk, he was known as "the headmaster" for good reason. Suspicious to the point of paranoia, he focused tenaciously on the past as justification for current actions. To the mystification of Western observers, Mugabe remained ideologically popular in the region and in wider Africa as a veteran liberation leader and Afronationalist. His repeated denunciations of neocolonialists earned him sincere admiration for "standing up" to Western hectoring. There is an important rationale to this: What, after all, was independence if not total equality and entitlement, and a refusal to be browbeaten by former colonial oppressors?

In November 2017, the oldest and third-longest-serving world leader finally stepped down, leaving Zimbabwe with multiple challenges. Complex and deep-seated problems associated with the long-term damage of a fractured political movement left a dubious legacy within ZANU-PF and in its relationship with the military and the security apparatus, riven by differing affiliations. These problems within the country's power structures and elites combined with a squabbling proliferation of political parties, a compromised judiciary, and hollowed-out state institutions in which the security forces control key levers of power—arguably, challenges comparable to those Mugabe himself faced on coming to office in April 1980. His successor is confronted with a liquidity crisis, massive debt arrears (estimated at approximately $9–10 billion), bloated cabinet and civil service spending, grossly inefficient parastatal organizations, huge structural unemployment, and endemic corruption that is now embedded in wider society. And having gone back to the barracks, will the military indeed stay there?

The new president and head of ZANU-PF, Emmerson Mnangagwa, is likely to have a short "honeymoon." As the 2013 Constitution requires the next elections to be held by August 2018, there is particular pressure to deliver results to underpin his legitimacy. But there still remains residual strength in the Zimbabwean political economy: its human skills capacity, a preexisting government strategy to reengage with the international community and domestic business, an entrepreneurial and engaged diaspora, and considerable goodwill. Time will tell whether President Mnangagwa can satisfy his core constituencies in ZANU-PF, the security apparatus and the war veterans, and the enormous weight of expectation within wider Zimbabwean society.

Robert Mugabe strove for the radical transformation of his country, yet came to be regarded as the principal author of Zimbabwe's current troubles. This is simplistic, but as leader he cannot completely escape this damning indictment. Longevity in office proved a Greek tragedy for Mugabe as a man and a leader, and for his country.

Sir J. Willoughby   Lady A. Poulett   Capt Villiers   Hon. R. White   Lord Annaly
R.H.G.   R.H.G.   R.A.   Hon. C. White
         Lord H. Poulett Hon. A. White Capt Vincent Smith

Bulawayo. Matabeleland. S.Africa. August 26th 1895.

1. Aristocratic members of the Pioneer Column sent by Cecil
Rhodes to colonize the country, many of whom became large
landowners, Bulawayo, August 26, 1895. Collection of Martin
Plaut.

2. Chiefs Babyom and Omjaam, senior counselors of the Matabele king, Lobengula, captured during the Matabele wars. They had previously been sent to England to petition Queen Victoria. Collection of Martin Plaut.

3. Ndebele men and women captured during the Second
Matabele War (1896–97), part of the first Chimurenga.
Collection of Martin Plaut.

4. Front cover of Rhodesian propaganda brochure distributed in the country and South Africa to bolster support for the white minority government led by Ian Smith. Rhodesian government document.

5. Robert Mugabe and Joshua Nkomo at an early session of the Rhodesia Constitutional Conference, Lancaster House, London, 1979. Commonwealth Secretariat.

6. Prime Minister Robert Mugabe of Zimbabwe, addressing a press conference, Commonwealth Heads of Government Meeting, New Delhi, 1983. Commonwealth Secretariat.

7. President Robert Mugabe and HM Queen Elizabeth II, Commonwealth Heads of Government Meeting, Harare, 1991. Commonwealth Secretariat.

8. Presidents Robert Mugabe of Zimbabwe, Nelson Mandela of South Africa, and Sam Nujoma of Namibia at the Commonwealth Heads of Government Meeting, Auckland, 1995. Commonwealth Secretariat.

9. A farm in southeastern Zimbabwe given to landless people as part of the land redistribution program. Collection of Martin Plaut.

10. Demonstrations by Mugabe's critics outside the
Zimbabwe Embassy, London 2016. Zimbabwe Vigil.

Notes

Introduction

1. The Zimbabwe African National Union (ZANU) contested the 1980 elections under the title ZANU-PF (ZANU–Popular Front). The liberation movement/party has retained this title ever since.

Chapter 1: Controversial and Divisive Leader

1. Martin Meredith, *Mugabe: Power, Plunder, and the Struggle for Zimbabwe* (New York: Public Affairs, 2007), 15.

2. David Smith, *Guardian,* July 15, 2015.

3. The term Front Line States (FLS) refers to those countries bordering apartheid South Africa, who opposed its system of formal racial discrimination before 1994.

4. Available at http://thecommonwealth.org/history-of-the -commonwealth/harare-commonwealth-declaration, accessed July 7, 2017.

5. For example, the private conversation between Prime Minister Margaret Thatcher and Secretary General of the Commonwealth Shridath Ramphal at the Lusaka heads of government meeting in August 1979: "You realize, of course, that we have given it to the communist," Thatcher observed. "He is a nationalist mainly," Ramphal replied. Shridath Ramphal, *Glimpses of a Global Life* (Hertfordshire: Hansib, 2014), 362.

6. Ken Flower, *Serving Secretly—An Intelligence Chief on Record: Rhodesia into Zimbabwe, 1964 to 1981* (London: John Murray, 1987), 273.

7. Somerville, *Africa's Long Road since Independence: The Many Histories of a Continent* (London: Hurst, 2015), 97.

8. T. Mkandawire, "African Intellectuals and Nationalism," paper presented at CODESRIA's 30th Anniversary Conference, "Intellectuals, Nationalism and Pan-African Ideal," Dakar, Senegal, December 2003, 1–23; and Krista Johnson, "Whither Nationalism? Are We Entering an

Era of Post-nationalist Politics in Southern Africa?," *Transformation* 58 (2005): 1–19, quoted in Sabelo Ndlovu-Gatsheni, "Africa for Africans or Africa for 'Natives' Only? 'New Nationalism' and Nativism in Zimbabwe and South Africa," *Africa Spectrum* 44, no. 1 (2009): 61–78.

9. Ndlovu-Gatsheni, "Africa for Africans."

10. This mirrors the "patriotic whiteness" of the Rhodesian UDI period. Knox Chitiyo, seminar, London School of Economics, November 6, 2007.

11. Ndlovu-Gatsheni, "Africa for Africans." See also Sabelo J. Ndlovu-Gatsheni, "Making Sense of Mugabeism in Local and Global Politics: 'So Blair, Keep Your England and Let Me Keep My Zimbabwe,'" *Third World Quarterly* 30, no. 6 (2009): 1139–58. And Sabelo J. Ndlovu-Gatsheni, ed., *Mugabeism? History, Politics and Power in Zimbabwe* (New York: Palgrave Macmillan, 2015).

12. R. W. Johnson, "Reporter-at-Large: Tracking Terror through Africa: Mugabe, Qaddafi and Al-Qaeda," *National Interest*, no. 75 (Spring 2004): 161–72. See also R. W. Johnson, http://www.politicsweb.co.za /news-and-analysis/mugabe-gaddafi-and-alqaeda, accessed July 27, 2017.

13. "Zimbabwe's Mugabe Becomes African Union's Chairman," *Financial Times*, January 30, 2015.

14. "Mugabe Donates $1m to African Union," Reuters, July 3, 2017.

15. Bishop Abel Muzorewa, *Rise Up and Walk: An Autobiography* (London: Sphere Books, 1978), 141.

16. David Owen, *Time to Declare* (London: Penguin, 1992), 301.

17. Robin Renwick, *Unconventional Diplomacy in Southern Africa* (Basingstoke: Macmillan, 1997), 10.

18. Lord Carrington, *Reflect on Things Past: The Memoirs of Lord Carrington* (London: William Collins, 1988), 298.

19. Ngwabi Bhebe, *The ZANU and ZAPU Guerrilla Warfare and the Evangelical Lutheran Church in Zimbabwe* (Gweru: Mambo Press, 1999), 259.

20. Douglas Brinkley, ed., *The Reagan Diaries* (New York: Harper-Collins, 2007), 179.

21. Ali Mazrui, quoted in Chris Sanders, "Leadership and Liberation," in *Leadership in Colonial Africa: Disruption of Traditional Frameworks and Patterns*, ed. Baba Galleh Jallow (New York: Palgrave Macmillan, 2014), 140.

22. In 1994, Mugabe was made a Knight Commander of the Order of the Bath by the queen. He was stripped of this honor in 2008.

23. Eliakim M. Sibanda, *The Zimbabwe African People's Union, 1961–87: A Political History of Insurgency in Southern Rhodesia* (Trenton, NJ: Africa World Press, 2005), 86.

24. Ibbo Mandaza, "Will ZANU-PF Survive?," in *The Day after Mugabe: Prospects for Change in Zimbabwe,* ed. Gugulethu Moyo and Mark Ashurst (London: Africa Research Institute, 2007), 39–45.

25. Private information. Sally Mugabe was deeply mourned by Zimbabweans, who regarded her as one of the few people in high positions who refused to allow their relatives to enrich themselves, and who personally was not easily corrupted. Fay Chung, *Reliving the Second* Chimurenga: *Memories from Zimbabwe's Liberation Struggle* (Stockholm: Nordic Afrika Institute, 2006), 184.

26. Martin Rupiya, "The Call to the Generals," in Moyo and Ashurst, *Day after Mugabe*, 62–67.

27. Sara Dorman, *Understanding Zimbabwe: From Liberation to Authoritarianism and Beyond* (London: C. Hurst, 2016), 3.

Chapter 2: Birth of the Revolutionary

1. As an overall comparison, the Zezuru comprise approximately 18 percent of the black Zimbabwean population. Overall, chi-Shona-speaking communities made up 80 percent of Zimbabwe.

2. Reg Austin interview with Sue Onslow, December 3, 2016.

3. Peta Thorneycroft interview with Sue Onslow, December 6, 2016.

4. See Dorman, *Understanding Zimbabwe*, for the churches in post-1980 Zimbabwe.

5. Meredith, *Mugabe*, 22.

6. Sabelo Ndlovu-Gatsheni, "Dynamics of Democracy and Human Rights among the Ndebele of Zimbabwe" (PhD thesis, University of Zimbabwe, 2003), 60.

7. Lawrence Vambe, *From Rhodesia to Zimbabwe* (Pittsburgh: University of Pittsburgh Press, 1976), 101, quoted in Alois S. Mlambo, *A History of Zimbabwe* (Cambridge: Cambridge University Press, 2014), 133.

8. White emigration from the United Kingdom to Southern Rhodesia formed part of an accelerated flow of white economic migrants around Southern Africa in this period. See Josiah Brownell, *The Collapse of Rhodesia: Population Demographics and the Politics of Race* (London: I. B. Tauris, 2010).

9. Julian Manyon, "Zimbabwe—Mugabe's Gamble" (1981), Thames Television, *TV Eye*, https://www.youtube.com/watch?v=HyL0w7iCadU.

10. Sean O'Grady, "Robert Mugabe: The Dictator Bucking Zimbabwean Life Expectancy Rates," *Independent*, February 19, 2016.

11. Mlambo, *History of Zimbabwe*, 182.

12. Brian Raftopoulos and Alois Mlambo, eds., *Becoming Zimbabwe: A History from the Pre-colonial Period to 2008* (Harare: Weaver Press, 2009), 107.

13. The debate over the reasons for the split remains unresolved. Nathan Shamuyarira claims it was principally over Nkomo's determination to establish a government in exile, whereas Sithole and Mugabe argued it was more important to concentrate on party organization at home

(Raftopoulos and Mlambo, *Becoming Zimbabwe,* 112). Herbert Chitepo was elected national chairman of ZANU in 1964. Chitepo became chairman of Dare reChimurenga (ZANU's revolutionary council), which directed the war until 1975. Chitepo transformed ZANU into a Marxist-Leninist organization (in theory) and oversaw the shift to guerrilla warfare following the failure of the 1969–70 military strategy.

14. Document 394, DO 154/94, 5 September 1964, *British Documents on the End of Empire, Series B Volume 9, Central Africa,* ed. Philip Murphy, *Part II, Crisis and Dissolution 1959–1965,* ICWS, University of London (hereafter *BDEE).*

15. Documents 380, notes, referring to the copy in CAB 21/5064; 394, DO 154/94, 5 September 1964, *BDEE.*

16. Document 394, DO 154/94, 5 September 1964, *BDEE.*

17. Typically, Mugabe raised the issue of a more intensive program of education and training for Africans. Document 202, PREM 13/543, 27 October 1965, *British Documents on the End of Empire, Series A Volume 5, East of Suez and the Commonwealth 1964–1971, Part II, Europe, Rhodesia, Commonwealth,* ed. S. R. Ashton and William Roger Louis.

18. Interview with Joshua Nkomo, *End of Empire,* Chapter 14: "Rhodesia" (1985), Granada Television, https://www.youtube.com/watch?v=0DuNhsLR9y0.

19. See Richard Coggins, "Rhodesian UDI and the Search for a Settlement, 1964–1968, Failure of Decolonisation" (PhD thesis, University of Oxford, 2002).

20. Document 394, *BDEE.*

21. Richard Mobley, "The Beira Patrol: Britain's Broken Blockade against Rhodesia," *Naval War College Review* 55, no. 1 (Winter 2002): 63–84.

22. Wilfred Mhanda, interview with R. W. Johnson, "How Mugabe Came to Power," *London Review of Books,* February 22, 2001.

23. Meredith, *Mugabe,* 4–5. Mugabe consistently combined his Marxist-Leninist beliefs with a recognition of the churches' role (Catholic and Evangelical Lutheran) as partners in struggle. However, there was a complicated historical relationship between the colonial state and the original land grants to mission churches which had dispossessed Africans. Bhebe, *ZANU and ZAPU Guerrilla Warfare,* 87.

24. Flower, *Serving Secretly,* 121.

25. Mhanda interview.

26. Ibid.

27. Ibid.

28. Peasant motivations for supporting the liberation struggle were many and various. See Norma J. Kriger, *Zimbabwe's Guerrilla War: Peasant Voices* (Cambridge: Cambridge University Press, 1992).

29. David Moore, "The Zimbabwe People's Army: Strategic Innovation or More of the Same?," in *Soldiers in Zimbabwe's Liberation War,* ed. Ngwabi Bhebe and Terence Ranger (London: James Currey, 1996), 86.

Chapter 3: From Freedom Fighter to President of a One-Party State

1. Sarah L. Kachingwe, *Sally Mugabe: A Woman with a Mission* (Zimbabwe Department of Information and Publicity, 1994).

2. This explains, in part, why the Anti-Apartheid Movement was wary of Mugabe. The AAM was very close to the ANC, which was itself aligned with the Soviet Union, rather than the Chinese, following the Sino-Soviet split of 1960.

3. *Zimbabwe News,* June 5, 1977, quoted in Ian Taylor, *China and Africa: Engagement and Compromise* (London: Routledge, 2006), 110.

4. See Keith Somerville, *Southern Africa and the Soviet Union: From Communist International to Commonwealth of Independent States* (London: Macmillan, 1993).

5. Heidi Holland, *Dinner with Mugabe: The Untold Story of a Freedom Fighter Who Became a Tyrant* (London: Penguin Books, 2008), 51.

6. Zvakanyorwa Wilbert Sadomba, *War Veterans in Zimbabwe's Revolution: Challenging Neo-colonialism and Settler and International Capital* (London: James Currey, 2011), 42.

7. Holland, *Dinner with Mugabe,* 50.

8. Bhebe, *ZANU and ZAPU Guerrilla Warfare,* 79–80. This echoes the South African ANC/SACP's ideological strategy of "National Democratic Revolution."

9. Sadomba, *War Veterans,* 46.

10. Edgar Tekere, in Holland, *Dinner with Mugabe,* 49–50.

11. Sadomba, *War Veterans,* 52.

12. Paul Moorcraft and Peter McLaughlin, *The Rhodesian War: A Military History* (Barnsley, UK: Pen and Sword, 2008), 85–86.

13. Quoted in Peter McLaughlin, *The Catholic Church and the War of Liberation,* 583, cited in Ngwabi Bhebe and Terence O. Ranger, eds., *Society in Zimbabwe's Liberation War* (Harare: University of Zimbabwe Publications, 1995), 24.

14. Zvakanyorwa Wilbert Sadomba, *War Veterans in Zimbabwe's Revolution: Challenging Neo-Colonialism and Settler and International Capital* (Harare: Weaver Press, 2011), quoted in Nyasha M. GuramatunhuCooper, "The Warrior and the Wizard: The Leadership Styles of Josiah Tongogara and Robert Mugabe during Zimbabwe's Liberation Struggle," in *Leadership in Colonial Africa: Disruption of Traditional Frameworks and Patterns,* ed. Baba G. Jallow (Houndmills, UK: Palgrave Macmillan, 2014), 103.

15. Mario Diani and Doug McAdam, eds., *Social Movements and Networks: Relational Approaches to Collective Action* (Oxford: Oxford University Press, 2003), quoted in Guramatunhu Cooper, "The Warrior and the Wizard," 104.

16. Chung, *Reliving the Second* Chimurenga.

17. See David Moore, "Democracy, Violence and Identity in the Zimbabwean War of National Liberation: Reflections from the Realms of Dissent," *Canadian Journal of African Studies* 29 (1995): 375–402.

18. See Sadomba, *War Veterans*, 47.

19. Owen, *Time to Declare*, 301.

20. Julian Amery, Conservative Party Conference, October 1979, *End of Empire*, Chapter 14, https://www.youtube.com/watch?v=0DuNhsLR9y0.

21. Carrington, *Reflect*, 295.

22. Peter Petter-Bowyer, *Winds of Destruction* (Victoria, Canada: Trafford, 2003), 511. The Rhodesian SAS speculated that Mugabe had been forewarned by a British secret service mole within the CIO in Salisbury.

23. Professor Reg Austin, ZAPU legal adviser, Lancaster House negotiations, interview with Sue Onslow, November 3, 2016.

24. Renwick, *Unconventional Diplomacy*, 12.

25. Jeffrey Davidow, *A Peace in Southern Africa: The Lancaster House Conference on Rhodesia, 1979* (Boulder, CO: Westview Press, 1984); Renwick, *Unconventional Diplomacy*.

26. Carrington, *Reflect*, 295.

27. Moorcraft and McLaughlin, *Rhodesian War*, 41.

28. Moses Anafu interview with Sue Onslow, July 2013, www.commonwealthoralhistories.org.

29. Sue Onslow, "Zimbabwe: Land and the Lancaster House Settlement," *British Scholar* 2, no. 1 (September 2009): 40–75. There was keen British awareness of the central importance of the land question, both to Zimbabwean nationalism, and as developmental policy.

30. See Kriger, *Peasant Voices;* and Jocelyn Alexander, *The Unsettled Land: State-Making and the Politics of Land in Zimbabwe, 1893–2003* (Oxford: James Currey, 2006).

31. Michael Charlton, *The Last Colony in Africa: Diplomacy and the Independence of Rhodesia* (Oxford: Blackwell, 1990), 80.

32. Reports on Statements by ZANU, August 7/8, 1979, Radio Maputo, August 7, 1979, in *The Struggle for Independence, Documents on the Recent Development of Zimbabwe (1975–1980)*, ed. Goswin Baumhögger (Hamburg: Institut für Afrika-kunde, Dokumentations-Leitstelle Afrika, 1984), vol. 5, doc. 878d.

33. Quoted in Nancy Mitchell, *Jimmy Carter and Africa: Race and the Cold War* (Stanford, CA: Stanford University Press, 2016), 626.

34. Martyn Gregory, "The Zimbabwe Election: The Political and Military Implications" (based on Gregory's November 18, 1979, interview with Mugabe), *Journal of Southern African Studies* 7, no. 1 (1980): 22, cited in Mitchell, *Jimmy Carter and Africa*, 639.

35. *End of Empire*, Chapter 14.

36. William Depree, "US Ambassador in Mozambique," cited in Mitchell, *Jimmy Carter and Africa*, 642.

37. As the most prominent soldier on the ZANLA side, Tongogara had considerably more influence over ZANLA fighters than Mugabe did. Paul Moorcraft and Peter McLaughlin, *Chimurenga! The War in Rhodesia, 1965–1980* (Marshalltown: Sygma/Collins, 1982), 219–20. Tongogara was killed in a car accident in Mozambique on December 25, 1979. South African sources speculated this was a GDR contract killing. At Mugabe's request, the British arranged with the Rhodesians for Tongogara's body to be embalmed and taken to his birthplace near Selukwe for burial. Renwick, *Unconventional Diplomacy*, 69.

38. Prime Minister Thatcher persisted in viewing Mugabe as a Communist-inspired terrorist, and nearly refused to shake his hand at the conclusion of the Lancaster House talks. Charles Moore, *Margaret Thatcher* (London: Allen Lane, 2013), 1:503.

39. ZANLA owed its strength largely to seasoned FRELIMO fighters within its ranks. Therefore, Mugabe was faced with a weakened military, and no rear base havens. (Sibanda, *Zimbabwe African People's Union*, 219). Machel also strongly advised him to moderate his Marxist rhetoric in the ZANU election manifesto.

40. Vladimir Shubin, *The Hot "Cold War": The USSR in Southern Africa* (London: Pluto Press, 2009), 182.

41. See Sue Onslow, "The Man on the Spot: Christopher Soames and the Decolonisation of Zimbabwe/Rhodesia," *Britain and the World* 6, no. 1 (2013): 68–100.

42. Carrington, *Reflect*, 303.

43. See Moorcraft and McLaughlin, *Rhodesian War*, 177, for an outline of Operation Quartz; and 178–89. See also Holland, *Dinner with Mugabe*, for an account of the South African–backed coup attempt.

44. Emeka Anyaoku, *The Inside Story of the Modern Commonwealth* (Ibadan: Evans Brothers, 2004), 80.

45. Total casualties in the Rhodesian counterinsurgency/liberation war amounted to 1,047 members of the Rhodesian security forces, a third of whom were white; 481 white, Asian, and Coloured civilians were killed. Moorcraft and McLaughlin, *Rhodesian War*. Official Rhodesian figures put guerrilla fatalities at 8,250, and Zimbabwean civilian deaths at 691. Informed sources estimate that the actual number of deaths ranged between 30,000 and 80,000. Ian F. W. Beckett and John Pimlott, *Counter-insurgency: Lessons from History* (Barnsley, UK: Pen and Sword, 2011), 186.

46. Cephas G. Msipa, *In Pursuit of Freedom and Justice: A Memoir* (Harare: Weaver Press, 2015), 96.

47. *Chronicle (Bulawayo)*, April 18, 1980, cited in Mlambo, *History of Zimbabwe*, 195.

48. See Flower, *Serving Secretly*, 2–4.

49. Flower, *Serving Secretly*, 4, 273.

50. Flower's memoirs are matter-of-fact about the breakdown of relations between Mugabe, and Nkomo and his ZIPRA forces. "His policy of reconciliation [was] not fully reciprocated by some blacks and by many whites; but that was hardly his fault" (277–78).

51. *End of Empire*, Chapter 14.

52. Wilf Mbanga, first head of the Zimbabwe Information Service, and later editor of the opposition *Daily News*, and the *Zimbabwean*. Interview, Nehanda TV, http://nehandatv.com/tag/wilf-mbanga/.

53. Roadblocks witnessed by Martin Plaut.

54. Maurice Nyagumbo, in Manyon, "Zimbabwe—Mugabe's Gamble."

55. Bhebe and Ranger, *Soldiers in Zimbabwe's Liberation War*, 112–13.

56. Somerville, *Southern Africa and the Soviet Union*, 152, 154–55.

57. Reluctantly, Mugabe had invited a Soviet delegation to the independence celebrations; the fact that two Soviet representatives had been instrumental in refusing aid to ZANU underlined Moscow's insensitivity. Somerville, *Southern Africa and the Soviet Union*, 153. Whereas lowly ZANU officials met the Soviet delegates on arrival, the PRC's representative to the independence celebrations was met by Mugabe. The USSR only established diplomatic relations with Zimbabwe in 1981. To their chagrin, Western embassies were opened much more rapidly (Shubin, *The Hot "Cold War*," 187). Mugabe also gave permission for the CIA and M16 to bug the Soviet Embassy post-1982.

58. Another serious flaw was the issue of financial liabilities at independence: Mugabe's government inherited US$5.3 million multilateral debt, US$97.9 million bilateral debt, and private debt amounting to US$593.9 million. In 1980 over US$65 million was required in debt servicing alone. Under consistent pressure from international bankers, Mugabe agreed not to default. A political pattern emerged in which "Mugabe gives radical, anti-business speeches before government makes major pro-business decisions or announcements." Patrick Bond and Masimba Manyanya, *Zimbabwe's Plunge: Exhausted Nationalism, Neoliberalism and the Search for Social Justice* (Durban: University of Natal Press, 2002), 24–27.

59. Reg Austin to Sue Onslow, December 3, 2016.

60. Sadomba, *War Veterans*, 56.

61. Manyon, "Zimbabwe—Mugabe's Gamble."

62. Robert Mugabe interview, Thames Television's *TV Eye*, March 1983, https://www.youtube.com/watch?v=_Fk_bn-Ov00.

63. Robert Mugabe interview, Manyon, "Zimbabwe—Mugabe's Gamble."

64. Mbanga, interview, Nehanda TV.

65. Charles Moore, *Margaret Thatcher: The Authorized Biography* (London: Allen Lane, 2015), 2:76.

66. Catholic Commission for Justice and Peace in Zimbabwe, *Breaking the Silence: Building True Peace—A Report into the Disturbances in Matabeleland and the Midlands, 1980–1988* (Harare: Catholic Commission for Justice and Peace in Zimbabwe/Legal Resources Foundation, 1997).

Chapter 4: Refashioning the State, and the Hope of Multiracial Zimbabwe

1. Meredith, *Mugabe,* 79.

2. Electoral Institute of Southern Africa, *Zimbabwe: Print Media* (Johannesburg: South Africa, 2002), quoted in Blessing-Miles Tendi, *Making History in Mugabe's Zimbabwe* (Oxford: Peter Lang, 2010), 44.

3. Michael Bratton, *Power Politics in Zimbabwe* (Boulder, CO: Lynne Rienner Publishers, 2014), 61.

4. Ibid., 62.

5. Stephen Moyo, "Corruption in Zimbabwe: An Examination of the Roles of the State and Civil Society in Combating Corruption" (PhD diss., University of Central Lancashire, 2014), 176.

6. Ndlovu-Gatsheni, "Dynamics of Democracy," 68.

7. *The Cambridge History of Africa,* Vol. 5 (Cambridge: Cambridge University Press, 1976), 344 ff.

8. *The Cambridge History of Africa,* Vol. 6 (Cambridge: Cambridge University Press, 1985), 445 ff.

9. Meredith, *Mugabe,* 112–13.

10. Ian Scoones et al., *Zimbabwe's Land Reform: Myths and Realities* (Woodbridge: James Currey, 2010), 2.

11. Meredith, *Mugabe,* 120.

12. Alexander, *Unsettled Land,* 112–13.

13. The British did consider a compulsory land restitution program, but rejected it as covering too much of the country, and too expensive. London also wanted to keep white farming skills capacity in the country to help rebuild the economy postindependence, and to encourage white urban skills to stay too. It was also a policy designed to reassure South Africa.

14. Meredith, *Mugabe,* 119.

15. Scoones et al., *Zimbabwe's Land Reform,* 14.

16. Jocelyn Alexander, "State, Peasantry and Resettlement in Zimbabwe," *Review of African Political Economy* 21, no. 61 (September 1994): 335.

17. Meredith, *Mugabe,* 121.

18. All Party Parliamentary Group, *Land in Zimbabwe: Past Mistakes, Future Prospects* (HMSO, December 2009), 32.

19. Ibid., 34.

20. *Mail & Guardian,* December 22, 1997.

21. Dorman, *Understanding Zimbabwe,* 19.

22. David Martin and Phyllis Johnson, *The Struggle for Zimbabwe: The Chimurenga War* (London: Faber and Faber, 1981), 10.

23. Ibid.

24. Stephen Ellis, *External Mission: The ANC in Exile, 1960–1990* (London: C. Hurst, 2012), 134.

25. Mark Gevisser, *Thabo Mbeki: The Dream Deferred* (Johannesburg: Jonathan Ball, 2009), 431–46.

26. Merle Lipton, "Understanding South Africa's Foreign Policy: The Perplexing Case of Zimbabwe," *South African Journal of International Affairs* 16, no. 3 (December 2009): 331–46.

27. Thabo Mbeki Foundaton, "South Africa's Policy towards Zimbabwe—A Synopsis," http://www.mbeki.org/2016/04/08/south-africas -policy-towards-zimbabwe-a-synopsis/, accessed November 14, 2016.

28. David Blair, "Tony Blair Denies Asking South Africa to Help Overthrow Robert Mugabe," *Daily Telegraph,* November 27, 2013.

29. William Minter and Elizabeth Schmidt, "When Sanctions Worked: The Case of Rhodesia Re-examined," *African Affairs* 87, no. 347 (April 1988): 228.

30. See Chief Emeka Anyaoku interview with Sue Onslow, www .commonwealthoralhistories.org; and Gevisser, *Thabo Mbeki,* 302.

31. Stephen Chan, "Mbeki's Failure over Zimbabwe," *New Statesman,* April 23, 2008.

32. Don McKinnon, *In the Ring: A Commonwealth Memoir* (London: Elliot and Thompson, 2013), 162.

33. Chantelle Benjamin, "Khampepe: Zim's 2002 Elections Not Free and Fair," *Mail & Guardian,* November 14, 2014.

34. "Report on the 2002 Presidential Elections of Zimbabwe," http://cdn.mg.co.za/content/documents/2014/11/14/reportonthe-2002presidentialelectionsofzimbabwe.pdf.

35. See, inter alia: Gordon Corera, "MI6 and the Death of Patrice Lumumba," *BBC News,* April 2, 2013.

36. Gerard Prunier, *Africa's World War: Congo, the Rwandan Genocide, and the Making of a Continental Catastrophe* (Oxford: Oxford University Press, 2009).

37. Martin Rupiya, "A Political and Military Review of Zimbabwe's Involvement in the Second Congo War," in *The African States of the Congo War,* ed. John E. Clark (New York: Palgrave Macmillan, 2002), 96.

38. Ibid., 101.

39. Meredith, *Mugabe,* 148.

40. Wilson Johwa, "Zimbabwe's Secret War in the DRC," *Mail & Guardian,* September 11, 2004.

41. Rupiya, "Political and Military Review," 103.

42. Bratton, *Power Politics,* 195.

43. Dorman, *Understanding Zimbabwe,* 115 ff, has meticulously recorded the emergence of these trends.

44. Ibid., 102.

45. Ibid., 128.

46. Ibid., 155–56. See also Raftopoulos and Mlambo, *Becoming Zimbabwe;* and Stephen Chan, *Southern Africa: Old Treacheries and New Deceits* (New Haven, CT: Yale University Press, 2011).

47. "Mugabe Accepts Referendum Defeat," *BBC News,* February 15, 2000.

48. "Zimbabwe Crisis Summit," *BBC News,* April 20, 2000.

Chapter 5: Revolution Redux, or "Why It All Turned Sour"

1. Bratton, *Power Politics,* 75.

2. Sam Moyo and Paris Yeros, "Land Occupations and Land Reform in Zimbabwe: Towards the National Democratic Revolution," in *Reclaiming the Land: The Resurgence of Rural Movements in Africa, Asia and Latin America,* ed. Sam Moyo and Paris Yeros (London: Zed Books, 2004), 186.

3. Sam Moyo and Paris Yeros, introduction to *Reclaiming the Land,* 21–22.

4. Bond and Manyanya, *Zimbabwe's Plunge,* 274.

5. Michael Auret, *From Liberator to Dictator: An Insider's Account of Robert Mugabe's Descent into Tyranny* (Cape Town: David Philip, 2009), 155.

6. Meredith, *Mugabe,* 167.

7. Bratton, *Power Politics,* 76.

8. Allister Sparks, *Beyond the Miracle: Inside the New South Africa* (London: Profile Books, 2003), 320.

9. Scoones et al., *Zimbabwe's Land Reform.*

10. General Agricultural and Plantation Workers Union of Zimbabwe, *If Something Goes Wrong: The Invisible Suffering of Farmworkers due to "Land Reform"* (Harare: Weaver Press, 2010), 13.

11. Ibid., 23.

12. Sam Moyo, "Three Decades of Agrarian Reform in Zimbabwe," *Journal of Peasant Studies* 38, no. 3 (July 2011): 493–531.

13. Food and Agriculture Organization of the United Nations, GIEWS Country Briefs: Zimbabwe, June 27, 2017, http://www.fao.org/giews/countrybrief/country.jsp?code=ZWE.

14. Zimbabwe National Statistics Agency, "Facts and Figures," 2015, http://www.zimstat.co.zw/sites/default/files/img/publications/Prices/Fact_2015.pdf.

15. See, for example, Scoones et al., *Zimbabwe's Land Reform,* and Joseph Hanlon, Jeanette Manjengwa, and Teresa Smart, *Zimbabwe Takes Back Its Land* (Sterling, VA: Kumarian Press, 2013).

16. Scoones et al., *Zimbabwe's Land Reform,* 238 ff.

17. Ibid., 233.

18. Bloomberg News, "Rural Zimbabwe Empties as Mugabe Land Reform Policy Unravels," *Bloomberg,* February 28, 2017.

19. Dorman, *Understanding Zimbabwe,* 181.

20. Anna Tibaijuka, *Report of the Fact-Finding Mission to Zimbabwe to Assess the Scope and Impact of Operation Murambatsvina,* http://www.un.org/News/dh/infocus/zimbabwe/zimbabwe_rpt.pdf.

21. Dorman, *Understanding Zimbabwe,* 156.

22. Jonathan Crush, Abel Chikanda, and Godfrey Tawodzera, *The Third Wave: Mixed Migration from Zimbabwe to South Africa,* Southern African Migration Programme, 2012, Published by the Southern African Research Centre, Queen's University, Canada, and the Open Society Initiative for Southern Africa.

23. Ibid. Informal figures put the number closer to 2.5 million, with nearly 1 million of the best-trained members of the Zimbabwe middle class seeking economic and political asylum in the United Kingdom.

Chapter 6: "Look East" for Foreign Friends

1. Bratton, *Power Politics,* 88.

2. Ibid., 91.

3. Ibid., 138.

4. Ibid., 137.

5. Zhang Chun, *China-Zimbabwe Relations: A Model of China-Africa Relations?* South African Institute of International Affairs, Johannesburg, Occasional Paper 205, November 2014, p. 6.

6. Lindsey Hilsum, "Small Fish in a Chinese Sea," in *The Day after Mugabe: Prospects for Change in Zimbabwe,* ed. Gugulethu Moyo and Mark Ashurst (London: Africa Research Institute, 2007), 144.

7. Zhang Chun, *China-Zimbabwe Relations,* 7.

8. Dorman, *Understanding Zimbabwe,* 40.

9. Zhang Chun, *China-Zimbabwe Relations,* 16.

10. European Council, Council of the EU, "Zimbabwe: EU Extends Sanctions by One Year," press release, February 15, 2016, http://www.consilium.europa.eu/en/press/press-releases/2016/02/15-zimbabwe-eu-prolongs-sanctions-by-one-year/.

11. Peter Greste, "Civil Society's Triumph on Zimbabwe," *BBC News,* April 25, 2008.

12. Human Rights Watch, *Diamonds in the Rough: Human Rights Abuses in the Marange Diamonds Fields of Zimbabwe,* June 26, 2009, 12.

13. David Towriss, "Buying Loyalty: Zimbabwe's Marange Diamonds," *Journal of Southern African Studies* 39, no. 1 (July 2013): 101.

14. Human Rights Watch, *Diamonds in the Rough,* 14.

15. Ibid., 15.

16. Towriss, 107.

17. Ibid., 105.

18. Ibid., 110.

19. Global Witness, *Diamonds: A Good Deal for Zimbabwe?* London, February 13, 2012, https://www.globalwitness.org/en/reports/diamonds-good-deal-zimbabwe/.

20. James Mupfumi, "Alluvial Diamond Mining in Marange," Country Report, May 2015, http://docplayer.net/24585331-Country-report-alluvial-diamond-mining-in-marange.html.

21. Zhang Chun, *China-Zimbabwe Relations,* 17.

22. Global Witness, *Diamonds.*

23. Ibid.

24. Annina Kärkkäinen, "Does China Have a Geoeconomic Strategy towards Zimbabwe? The Case of the Zimbabwean Natural Resource Sector," *Asia-Europe Journal* 14, no. 2 (November 2015): 185–202.

25. Peta Thornycroft, "Secret Airstrip Built at Zimbabwe Diamond Field," *Daily Telegraph,* January 31, 2010.

26. Towriss, "Buying Loyalty," 112.

27. "The key management of these companies is drawn primarily from serving or retired senior Chinese and Zimbabwean military personnel." Crispen Chinguno, Taurai Mereki, and Nunurayi Mutyanda, "Chinese Investments, Marange Diamonds and 'Militarised Capitalism' in Zimbabwe," *Global Labour Column* (University of the Witwatersrand), no. 200 (May 2015), http://column.global-labour-university.org/2015/05/chinese-investments-marange-diamonds.html.

28. Towriss, "Buying Loyalty," 113.

29. Peta Thornycroft, "Mugabe's Wife to Move into White Couple's Farm," *Telegraph,* August 20, 2002.

30. David Pallister, "International Hunt for Mugabe Family Assets," *Guardian,* January 16, 2002.

31. Itai Mushekwe, "Mugabe Assured of Malaysia Safe Haven," *Nehabda Radio,* March 25, 2013.

32. Peta Thornycroft, "Grace Mugabe, the Businessman and the Hong Kong Villa," *Telegraph,* May 24, 2015.

33. Andrew Malone, *Daily Mail,* December 12, 2014.

34. "Bob's 2016 Travels: The Map and the Millions," *New Zimbabwe,* December 23, 2016.

35. Frank Chikowore, "Mugabe, 92, Splashes Millions on Holiday as Zimbabweans Starve," *News24,* December 22, 2016.

Chapter 7: Mugabe and the People

1. Obonye Jonas, David Mandiyanike, and Zibani Maundeni, "Botswana and Pivotal Deterrence in the Zimbabwe 2008 Political Crisis," *Open Political Science Journal* 6 (2013): 1–9.

2. Bridget Mananavire, "Mugabe Clocks Up 220,000km Flying," *Daily News,* July 6, 2015.

3. "Zimbabwe Stands Still as President Vacations Off the Grid," *New York Times,* January 26, 2017.

4. David Coltart, *The Struggle Continues: 50 Years of Tyranny in Zimbabwe* (Johannesburg: Jacana Media, 2016), 492.

5. Hanlon, Manjengwa, and Smart, *Zimbabwe Takes Back Its Land,* 209.

6. Ibid., 192.

7. Ian Scoones, "What Happened to Farm Workers following Zimbabwe's Land Reform?," *Zimbabwean,* December 7, 2015.

8. Rodrigo, "What Happened to Comercial [*sic*] Farm Workers after the Famous Land Reform (Grab) Programme in Zimbabwe?," *WritePass Journal,* October 24, 2016.

9. Christopher Mahove, "Zimbabwe: Displaced Farm Workers Face Crisis," *Equal Times,* July 3, 2014.

10. Dorman, *Understanding Zimbabwe,* 194.

11. Zimbabwe Election Support Network, *Report on the 31 July 2013 Harmonised Elections,* http://www.zesn.org.zw/wp-content/uploads/2016/04/ZESN-2013-harmonised-election-report.pdf.

12. "Zimbabwe Election: A Guide to Rigging Allegations," *BBC News,* August 7, 2013.

13. Dorman, *Understanding Zimbabwe,* 197.

14. "Hot Seat Interview with Derek Matyszak on the Voters Roll," *Hot Seat with Violet Gonda,* February 24, 2017, http://www.violetgonda.com/2017/02/hot-seat-interview-with-derek-matyszak-on-the-voters-roll/.

15. John Makumbe, "Local Authorities and Traditional Leadership," in *Local Government Reform in Zimbabwe: A Policy Dialogue,* ed. Jaap de Visser, Nico Steytler, and Naison Machingauta (Harare: Community Law Centre, 2010), 88–100.

16. Ibid., 89.

17. Derek Matyszak, "Formal Structures of Power in Rural Zimbabwe," Commercial Farmers Union of Zimbabwe, Research and Advocacy Unit, February 2011, http://www.swradioafrica.com/Documents/Formal%20Structures%20of%20Power%20in%20Rural%20Zimbabwe.pdf, accessed December 5, 2017.

18. Ibid.

19. Zimbabwe Election Support Network, *Report*.

20. Cris Chinaka, "Zimbabwe's Social Media Revolt Yet to Take Root in Rural Areas," *Reuters*, August 12, 2016.

21. BBC, "Zimbabwe Profile: Media," *BBC News*, November 21, 2017.

22. "How Many Zimbabweans Live in South Africa? The Numbers Are Unreliable," *Africa Check*, November 5, 2013, https://africacheck .org/reports/how-many-zimbabweans-live-in-south-africa-the -numbers-are-unreliable/.

23. Deborah Budlender, "Labour Migration by Numbers: South Africa's Foreign and Domestic Migration Data," MiWORC Fact Sheet No. 1, July 2013, Migrating for Work Research Consortium, University of the Witwatersrand, http://www.miworc.org.za/docs/MiWORC -FactSheet_1.pdf.

24. Elinor Sisulu, Bhekinkosi Moyo, and Nkosinathi Tshuma, "The Zimbabwean Community in South Africa," in *State of the Nation: South Africa 2007*, ed. Sakhela Buhlungu, John Daniel, Roger Southall, and Jessica Lutchman (Cape Town: HSRC, 2007), 555.

25. "Zimbabwe: Diaspora Remittances Down 12,5 Percent to U.S.\$704 Million in Year to November," *AllAfrica*, December 24, 2016, http://allafrica.com/stories/201612300115.html.

26. Jonathan Crush and Sujata Ramachandran, *Xenophobic Violence in South Africa: Denialism, Minimalism, Realism*, Southern African Migration Programme, 2014, University of Cape Town.

27. "South Africa Army Mobilises to Quell Mob Violence," *AFP*, May 22, 2008, https://web.archive.org/web/20080611092810/http://afp .google.com/article/ALeqM5gzax3SXQ8v0UUA6ydLpCsuHeCinA.

28. Blessing Vava, "South Africa's Silence on Zimbabwe Instrumental in Xenophobic Attacks," *Guardian*, April 29, 2015.

29. "We Must Follow Zimbabwe Model—ANCYL," *PoliticsWeb*, April 8, 2010, http://www.politicsweb.co.za/party/we-must-follow-zimbabwe -model--ancyl.

30. "Zimbabwe: Malema Describes Mugabe's Violent Landgrab as 'Opportunistic,'" *NewZimbabwe.com*, November 26, 2015.

31. "Malema tells Zimbabwe's Robert Mugabe to Go, and Enjoys Another Anti-white Rant," *TimesLive*, December 2, 2016, http://www .dispatchlive.co.za/politics/2016/12/02/malema-tells-zimbabwes -robert-mugabe-to-go-and-enjoys-another-anti-white-rant/.

32. Joann McGregor, "The Politics of Disruption: War Veterans and the Local State in Zimbabwe," *African Affairs* 101 (2002): 9–37.

33. "Zimbabwe War Veterans Denounce 'Dictatorial' Mugabe," *Al Jazeera*, July 21, 2016.

34. "Comment: This Is Not the Way of the Soldier," *Herald*, July 23, 2016.

35. "Zimbabwe: War Veterans Arrested for 'Insulting Mugabe,'" *Al Jazeera*, August 2, 2016.

36. "Hot Seat: Mugabe Is No Comrade Says War Vet Leader Douglas Mahiya," *Zimbabwean*, August 17, 2016.

Chapter 8: The Battles for Succession and Control of Levers of Power

1. Southall, *Liberation Movements*, 247.

2. David Compagnon, *A Predictable Tragedy: Robert Mugabe and the Collapse of Zimbabwe* (Philadelphia: University of Pennsylvania Press, 2010), cited in Southall, *Liberation Movements*, 248.

3. See Meredith, *Mugabe*, 81.

4. ACR 1982–83, B883, cited in Southall, *Liberation Movements*, 249.

5. "Zanu (PF) Has Eaten Its Own Sons," *Zimbabwean*, August 14, 2014.

6. Southall, *Liberation Movements*, 253.

7. Ibid., 255.

8. Ibid., 256.

9. Ibid., 259.

10. Former finance minister Tendai Biti interview with Violet Gonda: "Hot Seat: Biti Says Mugabe Takes at Least $4million on Every Foreign Trip," *HotSeat with Violet Gonda*, June 6, 2017, http://www.violetgonda.com/2017/06/hot-seat-biti-says-mugabe-takes-at-least-4million-on-every-foreign-trip/.

11. "ZANU-PF Courts Big Business ahead of Elections," http://newsdzezimbabwe.wordpress.com/2010/12/10/zanu-pf-courts, accessed February 22, 2017.

12. I am grateful to a former UN staff member posted to Zimbabwe for these observations.

13. Chung, *Reliving the Second Chimurenga*, 187.

14. Philip Barclay, *Zimbabwe: Years of Hope and Despair* (London: Bloomsbury, 2010), 48. Barclay was a British diplomat based in Harare between 2006 and 2009.

15. Dorman, *Understanding Zimbabwe*, 187.

16. Barclay, *Zimbabwe*, 92–94.

17. The Joint Operations Command (JOC), comprising the security chiefs, represents the ZANU-PF hardliners.

18. Dorman, *Understanding Zimbabwe*, 193.

19. Heidi Holland, quoted in Paul Moorcraft, *Mugabe's War Machine* (Barnsley, UK: Pen and Sword, 2011), 195.

20. Norma Kriger, "ZANU-PF Politics under Zimbabwe's 'Power-Sharing' Government," 13, cited in Dorman, *Understanding Zimbabwe*, 208. The former military commander of ZIPRA, and Home Affairs minister, Dabengwa split from ZANU-PF and revived his old party in 2008.

21. Gibbs Dube, "Will Mugabe Succession Fights Lead to Civil War in Zimbabwe?," *VOA Zimbabwe,* February 20, 2016, https://www.voazimbabwe.com/a/is-zimbabwe-on-brink-of-civil-war/3199533.html.

22. Former army commander and ZANU-PF powerbroker Solomon Mujuru was a leading Zezuru figure in the coterie surrounding Mugabe. One of the wealthiest men in Zimbabwe, he had substantial business interests and had benefited greatly from defense procurement contracts. He represented a key link in the president's chain of command with the army leadership, former guerrilla leaders, and junior officer corps, as well as a vital part of the president's patronage network. His death in 2011, in deeply mysterious circumstances, deprived his wife of considerable political leverage within the ZANU-PF Politburo. See Somerville, *Africa's Long Road to Independence,* 288.

23. Alan Cowell, "In Zimbabwe's Succession Battle, Mugabe Pulls the Strings," *New York Times,* November 21, 2014.

24. "The Mugabe Brawl," *Economist,* October 30, 2014.

25. As Grace Mugabe was awarded a PhD in sociology after only three months of formal registration, her nicknames now include "Amazing Grace."

26. "Freedom in the World 2016: Zimbabwe," *Freedom House,* https://freedomhouse.org/report/freedom-world/2016/zimbabwe, accessed February 23, 2017.

27. Gibbs Dube, "Generation 40 Causing Havoc in Mugabe's Faction-Riddled Zanu PF," *VOA Zimbabwe,* October 8, 2016.

28. Brian Raftopoulos, "The Persistent Crisis of the Zimbabwean State," *Solidarity Peace Trust,* June 9, 2016.

29. "'Name Your Successor,' Wife Urges Zimbabwe's Ageing Mugabe," *Reuters,* July 27, 2017.

30. "Freedom in the World 2016: Zimbabwe."

31. Charles Mabhena, "Mnangagwa Sticks to Business; Overlooks Mugabe Succession War," *ZimNews,* February 2, 2017.

32. Dan Stannard, former CIO, interview with Sue Onslow, August 1, 2008.

33. "Mugabe Brawl."

34. David Pilling and Andrew England, "Mugabe Era Draws to an End but It Will Be No Ordinary Succession," *Reuters,* February 22, 2016.

35. Everson Mushava, "Mugabe Succession Shocker, *Standard,* January 15, 2017.

Chapter 9: Eaten by the Crocodile?

1. Alex T. Magaisa, "The Godfather Has Spoken—But Was It Much Ado about Nothing?," *Zimbabwe Independent,* February 26, 2016.

2. AFP, "Zim Ex-War Veterans Leader in Court for 'Insulting' Mugabe," *News24.com,* December 3, 2014.

3. Jason Burke, "Robert Mugabe Sacks Vice-President to Clear Path to Power for Wife," *Guardian,* November 6, 2017.

4. Petina Gappah, "How Zimbabwe Freed Itself from Robert Mugabe," *New Yorker,* November 22, 2017.

5. MacDonald Dzirutwe, Joe Brock, and Ed Cropley, "'Treacherous Shenanigans'—The Inside Story of Mugabe's Downfall," Reuters Special Report, *Reuters,* November 26, 2017.

6. Bernard Mpofu and Elias Mambo, "Mnangagwe's Great Escape: The Details," *Zimbabwe Independent,* November 10, 2017.

7. Dzirutwe, Brock, and Cropley, "'Treacherous Shenanigans.'"

8. "The Crocodile Snaps Back," *Africa Confidential* 58, no. 23, November 17, 2017.

9. "Mugabe Drops the Crocodile," *Africa Confidential* 58, no. 23, November 10, 2017.

10. *Constitutive Act of the African Union,* July 11, 2000, http://www .achpr.org/files/instruments/au-constitutive-act/au_act_2000 _eng.pdf.

11. Father Mukonori was reported to be assisting in the mediation between the Zimbabwean military and the ninety-three-year-old president.

12. Jeffrey Moyo, "Robert Mugabe, in Speech to Zimbabwe, Refuses to Say If He Will Resign," *New York Times,* November 19, 2017.

13. Gappah, "How Zimbabwe Freed Itself."

14. "President Mnangagwa's Inauguration Speech in Full," *Chronicle,* November 25, 2017.

15. "Plundering of DR Congo Natural Resources: Final Report of the Panel of Experts (S/2002/1146)," *ReliefWeb,* October 16, 2002.

16. "Zimbabwe Officially Declares Mugabe National Holiday," *BBC News,* November 27, 2017.

17. "How Mugabe Ruined Zimbabwe," *Economist,* February 26, 2017.

18. Eddie Coss, personal communication, November 17, 2017.

19. Mondli Makhanya, "The Liberation Myth Is Busted," *News24,* November 6, 2017.

20. Source: Zimbabwe Infant Mortality Rate, 2017, *Geoba.se,* http:// www.geoba.se/country.php?cc=ZW.

Selected Bibliography

Abiodun, Alao. *Mugabe and the Politics of Security in Zimbabwe.* Montreal and Kingston: McGill-Queen's University Press, 2012.

Alexander, Jocelyn. *The Unsettled Land: State-Making and the Politics of Land in Zimbabwe, 1893–2003.* Oxford: James Currey, 2006.

Anyaoku, Emeka. *The Inside Story of the Modern Commonwealth.* Ibadan: Evans Brothers, 2004.

Auret, Michael. *From Liberator to Dictator: An Insider's Account of Robert Mugabe's Descent into Tyranny.* Cape Town: David Philip, 2009.

Bhebe, Ngwabi. *Simon Vengai Muzenda and the Struggle for the Liberation of Zimbabwe.* Gweru: Mambo Press, 2004.

———. *The ZANU and ZAPU Guerrilla Warfare and the Evangelical Lutheran Church in Zimbabwe.* Gweru: Mambo Press, 1999.

Bhebe, Ngwabi, and Terence Ranger, eds. *Society in Zimbabwe's Liberation War.* Harare: University of Zimbabwe Publications, 1995.

———, eds. *Soldiers in Zimbabwe's Liberation War.* London: James Currey, 1996.

Blair, David. *Degrees in Violence: Robert Mugabe and the Struggle for Power in Zimbabwe.* London: Bloomsbury, 2002.

Bond, Patrick, and Masimba Manyanya. *Zimbabwe's Plunge: Exhausted Nationalism, Neoliberalism and the Search for Social Justice.* Durban: University of Natal Press, 2002.

Booysen, Susan. "The Decline of Zimbabwe's Movement for Democratic Change-Tsvangirai: Public Opinion Polls Posting the Writing on the Wall." *Transformation: Critical Perspectives on Southern Africa* 84 (2014): 53–80.

Bratton, Michael. *Power Politics in Zimbabwe.* Boulder, CO: Lynne Rienner Publishers, 2014.

Brownell, Josiah. *The Collapse of Rhodesia: Population Demographics and the Politics of Race.* London: I. B. Tauris, 2010.

Carrington, Lord. *Reflect on Things Past. The Memoirs of Lord Carrington.* London: William Collins, 1988.

Chan, Stephen. *Citizen of Zimbabwe: Conversations with Morgan Tsvangirai.* Zimbabwe: Weaver Press, 2010.

———. *Robert Mugabe: A Life of Power and Violence*. London: I. B. Tauris, 2003.

———. *Southern Africa: Old Treacheries and New Deceits*. New Haven, CT: Yale University Press, 2012.

Charlton, Michael. *The Last Colony in Africa: Diplomacy and the Independence of Rhodesia*. Oxford: Blackwell, 1990.

Chung, Fay. *Reliving the Second Chimurenga: Memories from Zimbabwe's Liberation Struggle*. Stockholm: Nordic Afrika Institute, 2006.

Coltart, David. *A Decade of Suffering in Zimbabwe: Economic Collapse and Political Repression under Robert Mugabe*. Washington, DC: CATO Institute, 2008.

Davidow, Jeffrey. *A Peace in Southern Africa: The Lancaster House Conference on Rhodesia, 1979*. Boulder, CO: Westview Press, 1984.

Doran, Stuart. *Kingdom, Power, Glory: Mugabe, Zanu and the Quest for Supremacy, 1960–1987*. Midrand, South Africa: Sithatha Media, 2017.

Dorman, Sara. *Understanding Zimbabwe: From Liberation to Authoritarianism and Beyond*. London: C. Hurst, 2016.

Flower, Ken. *Serving Secretly—An Intelligence Chief on Record: Rhodesia into Zimbabwe, 1964 to 1981*. London: John Murray, 1987.

Hammer, Amanda, Brian Raftopoulos, and Stig Jensen, eds. *Zimbabwe's Unfinished Business: Rethinking Land, State, and Nation in the Context of Crisis*. Harare: Weaver Press, 2003.

Holland, Heidi. *Dinner with Mugabe: The Untold Story of a Freedom Fighter Who Became a Tyrant*. London: Penguin Books, 2008.

Jallow, Baba Galleh, ed. *Leadership in Colonial Africa: Disruption of Traditional Frameworks and Patterns*. New York: Palgrave Macmillan, 2014.

Kriger, Norma J. "ZANU-PF Politics under Zimbabwe's 'Power-Sharing' Government." *Journal of Contemporary African Studies* 30, no. 1 (2012): 11–26.

———. *Zimbabwe's Guerrilla War: Peasant Voices*. Cambridge: Cambridge University Press, 1992.

Lipton, Merle. "Understanding South Africa's Foreign Policy: The Perplexing Case of Zimbabwe." *South African Journal of International Affairs* 16, no. 3 (2009): 331–46.

Mandaza, Ibbo, ed. *Zimbabwe: The Political Economy of Transition, 1980–1986*. Dakar: CODESRIA, 1986.

Manyon, Julian. "Zimbabwe—Mugabe's Gamble." Thames Television, *TV Eye*, 1981.

Martin, David, and Phyllis Johnson. *The Struggle for Zimbabwe: The Chimurenga War*. London: Faber and Faber, 1981.

McKinley, Dale T. "South African Foreign Policy towards Zimbabwe under Mbeki." *Review of African Political Economy* 31, no. 100 (2004): 357–64.

Meredith, Martin. *Mugabe: Power, Plunder, and the Struggle for Zimbabwe's Future.* Oxford: Public Affairs, 2007.

Mlambo, Alois S. *A History of Zimbabwe.* Cambridge: Cambridge University Press, 2014.

Moorcraft, Paul. *Mugabe's War Machine.* Barnsley, UK: Pen and Sword, 2012.

Moorcraft, Paul, and Peter McLaughlin. *The Rhodesian War: A Military History.* Barnsley, UK: Pen and Sword, 2008.

————. *Chimurenga! The War in Rhodesia, 1965–1980.* Marshalltown: Sygma/Collins, 1982.

Moyo, Gugulethu, and Mark Ashurst, eds. *The Day after Mugabe: Prospects for Change in Zimbabwe.* London: Africa Research Institute, 2007.

Moyo, Sam, and Paris Yeros, eds. *Reclaiming the Land: The Resurgence of Rural Movements in Africa, Asia and Latin America.* London: Zed Books, 2004.

Msipa, Cephas G. *In Pursuit of Freedom and Justice: A Memoir.* Harare: Weaver Press, 2015.

Mugabe, Robert. *Our War of Liberation: Speeches, Articles, Interviews, 1976–1979.* Gweru: Mambo Press, 1983.

Muzorewa, Bishop Abel T. *Rise Up and Walk: An Autobiography.* London: Sphere Books, 1978.

Ndlovu-Gatsheni, Sabelo. "Africa for Africans or Africa for 'Natives' Only? 'New Nationalism' and Nativism in Zimbabwe and South Africa." *Africa Spectrum* 1 (2009): 61–78.

————. "Beyond Mugabe-Centric Narratives of the Zimbabwe Crisis." *African Affairs* 111, no. 443 (2012): 315–23.

————. "Dynamics of Democracy and Human Rights among the Ndebele of Zimbabwe." Unpublished PhD thesis, University of Zimbabwe, 2003.

————. "Making Sense of Mugabeism in Local and Global Politics: 'So Blair, Keep Your England and Let Me Keep My Zimbabwe.'" *Third World Quarterly* 30, no. 6 (2009): 1139–58.

————, ed. *Mugabeism? History, Politics and Power in Zimbabwe.* New York: Palgrave Macmillan, 2015.

Nkomo, Joshua. *The Story of My Life.* 2nd ed. Harare: SAPES Books, 2001.

Norman, Andrew. *Mugabe: Teacher, Revolutionary, Tyrant.* Staplehurst, UK: Spellmount, 2008.

————. *Robert Mugabe and the Betrayal of Zimbabwe.* Jefferson, NC: McFarland Publishers, 2004.

Owen, David. *Time to Declare.* London: Penguin, 1992.

Petter-Bowyer, Peter. *Winds of Destruction.* Victoria, Canada: Trafford, 2003.

Primorac, Ranka, and Stephen Chan, eds. *Zimbabwe in Crisis: The International Responses and the Space of Silence.* London: Routledge, 2007.

Raftopoulos, Brian, ed. *The Hard Road to Reform: The Politics of Zimbabwe's Global Political Agreement.* Harare: Weaver Press, 2013.

Raftopoulos, Brian, and Alois Mlambo, eds. *Becoming Zimbabwe: A History from the Pre-colonial Period to 2008.* Harare: Weaver Press, 2009.

Raftopoulos, Brian, and Ian Phimister, eds. *Keep on Knocking: A History of the Labour Movement in Zimbabwe, 1900–1997.* Harare: Baobab, 1997.

Ramphal, Shridath. *Glimpses of a Global Life.* Hertfordshire: Hansib, 2014.

Renwick, Robin. *Unconventional Diplomacy in Southern Africa.* Basingstoke: Macmillan, 1997.

Sadomba, Zvakanyorwa Wilbert. *War Veterans in Zimbabwe's Revolution: Challenging Neo-colonialism and Settler and International Capital.* Harare: Weaver Press, 2011.

Schoeman, Maxi, and Chris Alden. "The Hegemon That Wasn't: South Africa's Policy towards Zimbabwe." *Strategic Review for Southern Africa* 25, no. 1 (2003).

Scoones, Ian, et al. *Zimbabwe's Land Reform: Myths and Realities.* Woodbridge: James Currey, 2010.

Shubin, Vladimir. *The Hot "Cold War": The USSR in Southern Africa.* London: Pluto Press, 2009.

Sibanda, Eliakim M. *The Zimbabwe African People's Union, 1961–87: A Political History of Insurgency in Southern Rhodesia.* Trenton, NJ: Africa World Press, 2005.

Sithole, Masipula. *Zimbabwe: Struggles-within-the-Struggle.* Rujeko: Rujeko Publishers, 1979.

Sithole, Ndabaningi. *African Nationalism.* Cape Town: Oxford University Press, 1959.

Somerville, Keith. *Africa's Long Road since Independence: The Many Histories of a Continent.* London: Hurst, 2015.

———. *Southern Africa and the Soviet Union: From Communist International to Commonwealth of Independent States.* London: Macmillan, 1993.

Smith, Ian. *The Great Betrayal: The Memoirs of Africa's Most Controversial Leader.* London: Blake, 1998.

Tekere, Edgar Z. *A Lifetime of Struggle.* Harare: SAPES Books, 2007.

Tendi, Blessing-Miles. *Making History in Mugabe's Zimbabwe.* Oxford: Peter Lang, 2010.

———. "Robert Mugabe's 2013 Presidential Election Campaign." *Journal of Southern African Studies* 39, no. 5 (2013): 963–70.

Vambe, Lawrence. *From Rhodesia to Zimbabwe.* Pittsburgh: University of Pittsburgh Press, 1976.

Windrich, Elaine. "Then and Now: Reflections on How Mugabe Ruled Zimbabwe." *Third World Quarterly* 23, no. 6 (2002): 1181–88.

Youde, Jeremy R. "Why Look East? Zimbabwean Foreign Policy and China." *Africa Today* 53, no. 3 (2007): 3–19.

Index

207